Spindrift

Also by Zenda Vecchio and published by Ginninderra Press

Mavis

A Conversation with Emily

Children at the Gate

Tiger! Tiger!

Light on Dark Water

Becoming Kirsty-Lee

The Swan's Egg

Fractals (Pocket Poets)

Zenda Vecchio

Spindrift

Acknowledgements

The following stories have been previously published:
'Phone Box', *Tamba* 37; 'The Dam': *Island* 102; 'Blue Is For the Sky', *Tamba* 40;
'Portrait Mainly In Orange', *Polestar* 26; 'Oak', *Quadrant* September 2007;
'The Morning After', *Polestar* 21); 'White Bird', *Island* 123;
'Green Silk', *Wet Ink* 26; 'The Lady Medea', *Polestar* 24; 'Birds', *Polestar* 22;
'White Noise',: *Tamba* 51; 'Bless me, Father', *Tamba* 27;
'Play in Three Acts' (as 'On Thursday'), *Tamba* 35; 'The Trail Bike', *Tamba* 29;
'Birth of Sarah-Rose', *Tamba* 52; 'Andrzej', *Tirra Lirra* March 2003;
'Robbie', *Pendulum* 9; 'The Bear', *Goodnight, Goodnight*; 'Fulham Cove', Studio 104;
'Sylvia', *The Write Angle* March/April 2006; 'At the Beach', *FourW* 13;
'Brothers', *Quadrant* January/February 2000; 'Silences', *Pendulum* 8.

Spindrift
ISBN 978 1 74027 906 2
Copyright © text Zenda Vecchio 2015
Cover photo © Ginninderra Press 2015

First published in this form 2015 by
GINNINDERRA PRESS
PO Box 3461 Port Adelaide 5015
www.ginninderrapress.com.au

Contents

Phone Box

When Vanessa sees the phone box across the road, she stops. A sudden gust of wind blows the hair back from her face and she shivers and pulls up the collar of her jacket. Then, biting at her lip, she darts over and wrenches at the door. Her hands against the glass are so small they look like they belong to a child. She turns her head away quickly. All at once she can't bear to look at them.

Last year when they were still at high school, Sophie had been scathing about her hands. 'You'd think by now you'd have stopped biting your nails,' she'd said. Her own hands were beautiful and she'd spread them out for Vanessa to admire, so slender, her nails delicately coloured like the inside of an old shell.

'Elegant,' thought Vanessa and she'd ducked her head and concentrated on the poplar suckers coming up in the lawn.

Her hands were ugly. No matter what she did, they'd never look like Sophie's. Her hair over her face, she'd traced carefully around a little quivering poplar leaf. She didn't want Sophie to guess how she felt. Sophie knew too much already. She knew all the things Vanessa was careful not to tell her, all the things she didn't want anyone to know.

'But...but I was her friend,' whispers Vanessa now, staring at her hands on the phone box door. 'It was all right when it was other people. The things she knew about them and...and used. Davis and Lindsey and Mark, the things she said so they'd... And Davis had been going with Lindsey for nearly a year so he should have known better...' Vanessa lets go of the door so it slams shut again. She's suddenly doubtful. She wants to ring Sophie, she wants to tell her about Jason, Sophie's her friend but...

Vanessa pushes her clenched fist into her mouth. She's remembered Melbourne. That's when things began to change, that night at Aunt Min's, when Sophie said... But that's just it. Vanessa can't remember exactly what Sophie did say. She can only remember the sound of Sophie's voice and, inside herself, a choking sense of loss. Perhaps Sophie didn't say anything at all, not anything important; perhaps Vanessa only imagined it. Because last week, just last week, Sophie had caught up with her as they were coming out of Medieval History, caught up with her deliberately and begged her to join her for coffee in the refectory. Sitting across the table from one another, it was as if nothing had happened, Sophie's narrow, finely-boned face eager, intent. She'd started talking about the boys in her English tutorial, Nigel and Tony and the dark one, Stavros, has Vanessa noticed him, he never speaks, not to anyone, so of course he's more of a challenge but in the end, well, remember Davis, everyone thought he'd never… 'Succumb,' said Sophie. 'That's the word, isn't it, Vanessa? The perfect word.'

Vanessa had laughed and stirred more sugar into her coffee and all the time Sophie was talking, she'd watched her, watched her relieved, Sophie's eyes, her mouth, her eloquent, moving hands. But the next day, Sophie, passing with her new friends in the hall, had looked at Vanessa as if she had never seen her before, her eyes cool and remote, her lips curling with disdain.

Vanessa leans against the phone box and sighs. Melbourne. That's when it had changed, when they had gone to Melbourne to stay with Sophie's Great-Aunt Min. 'A reward,' Sophie had said with her secret smile. 'We need a reward for getting through Year Twelve.'

Only…only after the first day, Vanessa had begged Sophie to let her go home. It wasn't like she'd imagined. It was… 'Too much,' whispered Vanessa to herself. The stately old house. The immaculate gardens. The ornate furniture. The starched linen tablecloths. Perhaps those most of all.

'For just us?' stammered Vanessa, frowning.

'What is it, child?' said Sophie's aunt, smiling, gracious, extending a delicate hand. 'We're all the same, you know. We all bleed when we're cut.'

But Vanessa, lifting her eyes, knew for the first time that she and Sophie weren't the same, could never be the same because Sophie wanted this world, ached for it and she, Vanessa, didn't belong, could never belong…

But 'You can't go home,' said Sophie, furious. 'Don't be ridiculous. It would be so rude.'

So Vanessa waited. Ten days, only ten days. And in the end it was all right because Sophie took care of her. She was out of place, uncertain, a little staring schoolgirl but Sophie made it all right; Sophie knew all the proper things to say, to do, her friend Sophie. A dance of light. A silver shining. Whenever she looked at Sophie, that's what she saw, that's what she had always seen.

Then…then…the last night at Aunt Min's. Outside, in the darkness, Aunt Min's peacocks screaming on the lawn. Remembering, Vanessa starts to shudder as if she's back there again, listening.

Sophie's voice, light, casual, carefully cruel as they got ready for bed. 'You have to grow up, Vanessa,' she'd said. 'God knows I've tried hard enough to help you but you're still like Alice in Wonderland. All hair and eyes. You can't go on like that forever. Or maybe you can. I don't know. I don't care any more. I've had enough.'

'But…but…' Vanessa had cried, stricken. 'That's who I am and you said…you said…' Her voice broke and she turned her face away and whispered, 'You said you needed me. You said I was the only one who understood. You said when your image broke down, I was the only one who could help you put it together again.'

Sophie laughed. 'Image? Oh, that. It was a game. Don't you remember? Last year when I asked you to be friends with me, you didn't even know what an image was. Things are different now. In a few weeks, we'll be at university. We're too old for games and in any case I'm beginning to think, Vanessa, that you're nothing but a liability.'

Vanessa was glad then that Sophie had turned off the light. She'd started to cry, though she was careful not to make any sound. If Sophie knew she was crying, she'd laugh even more. She'd done that once at school, made Vanessa cry in front of everyone and then laughed. But this time it was different. Vanessa wasn't crying because of Sophie. She was crying for herself, for what she had just lost, the silver shining. She'd seen that right from the beginning, not Sophie, never just Sophie but the light, the light that shone around her.

Once she'd even tried to tell her. 'Oh,' she'd cried before she could stop herself. 'Oh, Sophie, I know what you're like. You're like the sun shining through droplets of water.'

Sophie, astonished, had stared at her for a moment but then her

9

expression had changed. 'Vanessa,' she said softly, 'Vanessa,' and she'd bent her head and started pleating the folds of her skirt. 'You know what your name means, don't you?' she'd said. 'Butterfly, it means butterfly, and I think, not now of course but one day, one day I think you will be just that, a butterfly.'

Her voice gave the word a sudden, lilting beauty so Vanessa could see herself in her own mind, a butterfly with jewelled wings. She felt her breath catch in her throat and Sophie, her face oddly gentle, leaned forward and let her fingers trail across Vanessa's cheek. Vanessa had turned away quickly. The feelings inside her were too much for her.

Now, remembering, Vanessa presses her hands against her throat. She wants to ring Sophie. Months, it's been months, and Sophie has repudiated her. But this is different. It has to be different. She needs Sophie. Perhaps it was just games before but now, Jason and what he's done is real and Sophie will understand, Sophie will help her bear it because Sophie knows all about boys.

And Sophie promised. Vanessa can remember that too. Sophie under the poplar trees at school, her face unexpectedly tender, 'Vanessa, oh, Vanessa, you're so innocent and you look it too and it won't always protect you. It…it frightens me. Promise me, promise me if you get into any trouble with boys, and you will, I know you will, promise me you'll tell me, you'll ring me up and tell me.'

Vanessa's crying now. She leans against the phone box and lets the hot tears slide down her cheeks. It isn't Jason, though. Suddenly he's stopped being important. It's Sophie. She's crying for Sophie, her friend Sophie who doesn't need her any more. She's crying because she wants to ring Sophie and she knows she can't.

The Dam

Now that she's seven, my sister Lani is a thin, ungainly little girl, all arms and legs and staring eyes. A spider, I think, and then I'm sorry, my throat starts to close up and I feel bad because Lani's all there is, all there'll ever be now and it has to be enough. And there's the other thing too, the thing that's Lani's alone. Pathos. That's my word for it. The pathos of her. All the little, helpless things; new grass after rain, the plaintive crying of a just-born lamb, the first tender leaves in spring, japonica, the blue wrens in the garden. They make my heart turn over. It isn't pity. Not exactly. But it's something like it. It's the only thing I feel now. The only thing that's real.

Joy and anger and grief. Love. Perhaps love most of all. They're just words. Perhaps that's all they ever were. I can't remember.

Except there's Lani. I've seen it in her face. Emotions. All the things I don't feel. It frightens me. I don't know why but now she's seven, I'm frightened for my sister Lani.

*

I'm not sure why I've started writing things in here. I've never liked writing things for school. Oh, it's all right when it's *Lord of the Flies* or *Hamlet* or even a description, 'View from a Window', I never minded that; I could write about the gums and the honeyeaters in the bottlebrush. *The banquet tree*, I wrote, *the bottlebrush outside my window is a banquet tree; all the birds come to it. This year, for the first time, I saw green musk lorikeets. Perhaps there's a drought inland...*

I'm in Year Twelve now. It's easier. There's not much time for creative writing, except once at the beginning of the year when Mr Marsden made us do an autobiography. I almost didn't do it. Once I started, though, I managed all right. It became a challenge.

My name is Alyssa Dixon and I'm seventeen years old. I live a fair way out of Stonyfell which means I have to catch the bus to school. Our property is called Redgums. We didn't name it. I think my grandfather did when he settled here. It sounds like something out of Enid Blyton... I had to stop for a moment then. It was getting too dangerous. Enid Blyton's so cosy. All those adventures but everyone's always safe. Julian, Dick, George and Anne. And Timmy the dog, of course. Especially, Timmy the dog. He'd never let anything happen to them, not dear old Timmy.

I bit my lip and started quickly on a description of my room. I was calm enough then to finish. The words almost wrote themselves. *I don't know what I'm going to do next year. Sometimes I think I would like to go to university and become a teacher but then I'd have to leave Redgums. I don't want to do that. It's too soon.*

Mr Marsden gave me a C-. I had to go and see him. He said he was disappointed in me. 'You haven't written about yourself,' he said. 'I can't get a picture of what you're like from this at all.'

I smiled then. I had to duck my head quickly so he wouldn't see. I couldn't help the smile, though. He's all right, Mr Marsden, a lot better than some of my other teachers, but I can't tell him about myself. I can't tell anyone and it's not only because I don't want them to know.

*

It's night. I wake up and my room is full of dark shadows. Outside the wind's come up. I hate the wind. It wants to get inside. It wants to...

Sobbing, I turn my head on the pillow. The wall. I face the other wall instead of the window. An animal. If only the wind were an animal. A panther. A bear. Snarl of teeth and yellow eyes. I sit up. That would be better. I'd be brave then. I could face it with clenched hands, my head up...

But...but...

The wind's got no shape. It's in the Bible. *The wind blows where it pleases. You hear its sound but you cannot tell where it comes from or where it goes.* Even before, I always hated it when they read that bit in church. It confused me. God and the wind. They sounded like the same thing. That's why I'm afraid of the wind now.

I don't go to church any more. None of us do. After Lani was born, the priest came around to make arrangements for her baptism.

Mum turned her head away. 'No,' she whispered. 'No, I don't believe in it now.' She tried to make herself smile but her eyes were still empty. 'It doesn't do any good,' she said. 'You must know that yourself. In the end, it doesn't make any difference.'

Father John would have argued but my father stood up. 'Perhaps you'd better go,' he said. 'You can see how it is with us. We've had enough of God.'

Father John's face flushed. 'Enough?' he said. 'What do you mean? No one can have enough of God.'

I can't forget that. At night when the wind hurls itself against my window, I hear his voice again. *Enough. Enough. No one can have enough of God.* And sometimes it isn't his voice. It's theirs.

Rain's all right, hail and sleet, even mist. I remember the mist rising from the dam in autumn; it was like smoke and the water below gleamed silver, so still you'd think you could walk upon it... I bite down hard on the inside of my lip until my mouth is full of the taste of blood.

I throw myself back against my pillow and put my hands over my ears. I force pictures into my mind. Other pictures. Safe pictures. The fire in the grate, the little flags of flame, they dance and leap and flutter, red and orange and sunshine-yellow. Mum coming in from the kitchen with a plateful of scones dripping with butter. Lani's thin little face as she lifts her head from her book, her lips still shaping the last silent word. The firelight catches itself in her hair so it glows copper, the colour of the poplar leaves in spring. I remember them too. The poplar tree by the paddock gate. It was just coming into leaf and I ran down and called out their names. It was too late, though. They wouldn't answer. They were angry with me and they wouldn't answer. Cameron and Rebecca and Miranda. Their names are in my mind. I hear them all the time but I won't let myself say them. Not now. Not now we've got Lani. When she was born, Mum said, 'Now we can begin again.' I want that too. I want that more than anything.

The wind's so loud. Even if they answered now, the wind wouldn't let me hear them.

'Please,' I whisper. 'Please stop.'

But the wind goes where it wants to. It doesn't care.

*

I've almost finished my chemistry assignment. It's due tomorrow. Lani comes in and stands by my desk. She jigs from one leg to the other. She wants to tell me something. I go on steadily with my work. When she's like this, it's best not to press her.

At last she's ready. 'I went down to the dam today,' she whispers.

My head jerks up. 'Lani…'

'I like it there. The water and then down by the overflow, the tamarisk trees. Pink. I never saw them like that before. All pink.'

'Lani, you know you're not allowed down there. You know…'

Her mouth goes stubborn. 'I don't care. I don't care what you say. I like it there.'

'Mum…

'Mum won't know. Not unless you tell her.' Suddenly her face changes, is soft, cajoling. 'Look, I brought you a tamarisk feather. It's special. You can have it for your desk.' When I don't answer, she lays the piece of tamarisk on my folder and pulls at my arm. 'You won't tell on me, will you, Allie? I didn't go near the edge. Honest.'

'You don't understand, Lani. It's not…it's not telling on you. It's…'

She stares at me a moment. 'I know why you don't want me to go there,' she says. 'I know everything.' Her voice doesn't sound right. It sounds triumphant.

Cameron…for a moment I think I see Cameron standing behind her. I shudder and close my eyes. I'm not sure how it's happened but I am back there and Cameron is twisting my arm up behind my back.

'She won't tell. She won't dare tell.' He jerks my arm harder. 'You won't tell, will you, Alyssa, because if you do…'

Rebecca's still not sure, though. She takes a step towards me. 'Oh, please come, Alyssa. It won't be the same without you. Cameron, I want her to come. Make her come too.'

I pull myself away from my brother. I'm panting as if I've been running. 'No. No, I won't come but I won't tell either. I promise I won't tell.' Then my eyes meet Cameron's. I make myself stand very tall. 'You're stupid,' I say. 'All of you. There isn't any magic kingdom under the water. There can't be. Rebecca…'

But I've lost her. She catches hold of Miranda's hand and faces me, suddenly defiant. 'You're scared. You're too scared to find out. Cameron's right. You're a baby.'

Before I can answer, Miranda interrupts. 'I'm not am I, Becky? I'm not a baby like Alyssa.'

14

Rebecca looks at me and her mouth twists. 'Course not, Miranda. I wish you were my twin instead of Alyssa.'

My breath catches in my throat with a sob. 'Lani,' I whisper. 'Lani, what is it you know?'

'I know about them. Cameron. Rebecca. Miranda. I know all about them.' Her lips start to quiver and to hide it she ducks her head and starts to play with the pencils on my desk. 'Why didn't you tell me about them, Alyssa? They belong to me too. Why didn't you tell me?'

For a moment, my mouth is so dry I can hardly speak. 'Lani, it was a long time ago. Before you were born and...' I stop then.

Lani's half-turned away from me. Her eyes are too big. They stare past me and I'm suddenly frightened at what they can see. Cameron... he said... But I could never understand the things he said. I thought he was making it up, the kingdom under the water. I know he was making it up. The shadows in the water. A trail of silver bubbles. A glow of light. Nothing. Nothing at all. But Rebecca and Miranda believed him. And Lani...Lani...

I jump up and grab her by the shoulders. I force her to look at me. 'Who told you?' I shout. 'Who told you about them? Come on. Tell me. Tell me the truth.'

'I...' She's flinching away but then her face crumples and she begins to whimper. 'I found... I was in the shed. The boxes there, I was looking for something to make a cloak for Princess Lobelia and...' She takes a choking breath and begins again. 'I found a lot of old photographs. Babies and...you...there were photos of you and some other children. They had names on the back and dates so I knew...and, and an old newspaper...it said...'

'I know what it said.'

Lani lifts her wet face. 'Why?' she whispers. 'Why did they drown in the dam, Alyssa? I went down there and there was nothing there except the water and the trees and the grass. And birds. I saw a lot of birds, little birds. They darted down to the water and then they...' She shakes her head. 'There wasn't anything else. I'm sure there wasn't. I liked it down there, really, Alyssa, but then the water... I saw something in the water and I wanted...'

I reach out and wrap my arms around her. She's so small. A bird, I think, my little sister's a bird, a blue wren perhaps or a little darting thornbill. 'There isn't anything else,' I whisper. 'How could there be? Oh, Lani, how could there be?'

But I'm lying. Even as I say it, I know I'm lying.

*

Now that Lani's said their names, it's like I can't stop thinking about them. My brother. My sisters. I see them in Lani's face. I don't want to but they are there all the same. Cameron's eyes. Miranda's smile. Even Rebecca.

I run to my mirror. 'Rebecca,' I whisper, staring at my reflection. If Rebecca were anywhere, surely it should be my face, my reflection looking back at me should be Rebecca's because…because… Twins. We were twins…

'I was scared,' I whisper to her. 'I was scared because I knew what would happen if you did what Cameron wanted and I…I was right.'

But it's my own eyes watching me. Rebecca isn't there. When I refused to go with them, I broke the connection between us.

'I didn't know,' I whisper desperately. 'I didn't know I'd be so lonely.' I grab the mirror with both hands and hold it very still. 'Rebecca, listen to me. Lani. You've got to make Cameron leave Lani alone. I know he's started on her just like he… Oh, Rebecca, he's got you and Miranda. You've got to make him leave me Lani.'

I stare hard at my own face. I want it to be Rebecca's as well. I want so much for her to understand.

*

It's summer. At the end of the day the little walled garden at the back of the house is full of the bruised scent of roses. I shudder and put out my hand to touch a little pink half-opened bud.

Lani's got her dolls spread out on the grass. She's telling them another story. 'And then the Princess Lobelia said, "Bring me back a pink feather from the tamarisk tree by the Dark Lake and it will be proof of your love." So the prince gets on his horse…'

No, no, I whisper to myself, it wasn't a tamarisk feather, it was a line of silver bubbles; they twisted and danced in the light…

16

I sigh. Something has happened to me. I've started to feel again. I look at Mum and Dad in case it's happened to them too. But they're just the same. Remote. Even when they smile, it isn't real. It isn't in their eyes. They're safe still. They don't know. They don't know about Cameron and Lani. I do, though. I watch her. I have to. Day after day, I watch her go down to the dam and stand there, staring at the water. It'll be harder for her. She's alone. She won't have Miranda and Rebecca to hold her hands.

*

Dawn. I wake up suddenly. It's very quiet. Outside, the sky is lemon-yellow. I stand at my window watching it. The little gum tree at the edge of the lawn glows with rosy, fairy lights. 'Christmas,' I say smiling, though I know it's just a trick of the light and they aren't real.

I pull on my jeans and T-shirt and go to wake up Lani. 'Come on,' I say, suddenly impatient. 'You've never been to the dam this early. Hurry up. I want to show you the light on the water.' I'm surprised at my own words. Until I said them, I didn't know that's where we were going. 'Cameron said there was a kingdom under the water, a magic kingdom, but only the valiant-hearted could find it.'

Lani's eyes go wide with wonder. 'Did you see it, Alyssa? Did you see Cameron's kingdom?'

'No. Not then. The others could but I...' For a moment my voice falters. Then I lift my head and look at her steadily. 'Maybe today, Lani. Maybe we'll find it today, together.'

'Oh, I hope so. I hope so.' She pauses, suddenly troubled. 'But you said I wasn't to go there. You said...'

'I was wrong.'

The feeling inside me's so strong I start to shudder with it. I wrap my arms around myself to hold myself still. In the mirror, behind Lani, I think I see Rebecca's eyes. They're smiling at me. After all this time, Rebecca's smiling at me.

My breath catches in my throat and I turn quickly to Lani. 'I know why I couldn't see it before,' I tell her. 'I had to wait for you.' I feel something break inside me and my eyes sting with tears. 'Come on. They're waiting for us, Cameron and Rebecca and Miranda. Oh, Lani, they're waiting for both of us.'

Lani's eyes meet mine and she nods solemnly. Then she laughs and grabs my hand and we run together through the silent, shadowy house and into sunshine outside.

Blue Is For the Sky

The goat's sick.

Emmie, lying on the kitchen floor drawing, carefully puts down her pencil. 'Why?' she asks. 'Why's Old Nannie sick?'

Mum's mouth goes tight. 'I don't know.' She puts the empty milk bucket on the table and sighs. 'Maybe she'll be better in the morning.'

All at once, Emmie doesn't want to draw any more. She sits up and smoothes her skirt over her knees. She doesn't like Old Nannie very much. None of them do. Obstreperous, that's what Grandad says – Old Nannie's obstreperous. Emmie's not at all sure what that means but she likes the sound of the word. It sounds like Old Nannie, obstinate and cross. It sounds like Old Nannie when Mum's milking her and she kicks over the bucket so the milk's all spilled and wasted.

'She'll get better, won't she?' she whispers. 'In the morning. She'll be better then, won't she, Mum?'

'I hope so. Otherwise I don't know what we'll do.'

But in the morning Old Nannie isn't better. Emmie, running ahead of Mum, stops at the gate. She can see Old Nannie lying by the side of the shed. She's not moving at all. Emmie puts her hand up to her mouth. She knows. Old Nannie looks asleep but she isn't. She's dead. The thing inside her that made her Old Nannie isn't there any more. It's gone away and nothing they can do will make it come back.

Emmie stares around her, bewildered. Everything's changed. The sky, the whispering grasses along the fence, the dam, the flowering tamarisk tree by the pump. Yesterday they were her friends, were part of all she knew. Now they've withdrawn from her. They're strangers like the rigid body of Old Nannie.

'Mummy,' whispers Emmie, pointing. 'Look. Look.'

Mum pushes past Emmie and opens the gate. 'Go back to the house.'

'But I…'

'Go on. Do as I say.'

But Emmie can't move. Her breath shudders in her chest and she reaches out to clutch at her mother's skirt. 'She's dead, isn't she? Old Nannie, she's…'

Mum turns to look at her. For just a moment, her eyes meet Emmie's and it's like they're sharing something, have reached an understanding, but then her mother's face changes, the hardness is back and the thin-lipped anger. 'Let go of me,' she hisses, jerking her dress free. 'What are you? A baby? I haven't time to bother with you now. Go on back to the house like I told you.'

Emmie turns and runs stumbling down the paddock. She's crying. It isn't Old Nannie. Or even Mum. She's used to Mum. It's something else. It's the whole world that's suddenly got too big. When she comes to the tamarisk tree, she hesitates. She loves the tamarisk tree. With a little cry of recognition, she flings herself under it and gives herself over to grief.

After a while, sensations come back. The rough grass under her cheek…the smell of damp leaves…birdsong…the plaintive bleating of a lost lamb. Emmie sits up and pushes her hair out of her eyes. Through the tamarisk branches, she can see bits of the sky, so soft and tender, the sky. And blue. The best colour. Blue, the colour she wants for herself. 'Like pink,' she whispers. 'Like pink is for the tamarisk tree.'

If Old Nannie had had a colour, she'd have been yellow. Emmie's sure of it. Obstreperous sounds yellow, as yellow as the flowers of the wild turnip that Old Nannie had liked best to eat. And her eyes. Old Nannie had narrow, yellow eyes that watched things scornfully as if she knew all their secrets and had long ago decided they were worthless.

Emmie takes a deep breath. It feels good giving Old Nannie her own colour. And Mum. What colour would Mum be? Frowning, Emmie bends down and picks up a small stone. Red perhaps, rust-red, because Mum's always so cross. Like when she saw Old Nannie was dead. She was cross with Emmie then, even though Emmie didn't want Old Nannie to be dead, even though…

Emmie bites at her lip and turns the stone around in her hands. She likes the way it glitters when it catches the light. Death, she thinks, shuddering, death is like that, all glittery, it takes things and changes them into something else, something different. Old Nannie's gone now. She's turned into something else. Not better or worse just…just different.

Emmie lies down again and pillows her head on her arms. She watches the sky through the branches of the tamarisk tree. It comforts her. 'Blue,' she whispers, her eyelids fluttering and beginning to close. 'I like blue best. I'll always like blue best because it's my colour.' The world has changed, Old Nannie is dead, but some things, the important things, have stayed the same.

Portrait Mainly In Orange

James has put little vases of nasturtium flowers all along the window ledge. Beneath them, on a wooden bench, there's a blue glazed bowl of citrus fruit. When she comes in with the rest of them, I wonder if it's deliberate. Her dress is the same colour, the only hint of brightness; the children are still in their school uniforms, even the little one's ribbons are grey, and Annie, of course, is in her usual dark blue. As soon as they're more or less seated, Claude shambles in; empty-eyed but as obedient as a dog, he takes his place by Leonardo and waits. It's like that now for him, I expect. Endless waiting.

She's like a bird. All tilted head and sharp-beaked profile. Not predatory, though. Not at all. Something else, something exotic. A sunbird perhaps. She accepts a chardonnay from James and then, holding the stem of the glass delicately between two fingers, amuses herself by twirling it round and round so it catches the light. They've told me about her of course but, seeing her like this, I'm sure they've haven't told me everything.

The children are all over Leonardo, the little one already on his lap. She's like Jackie, that one, same piquant face, and she knows, already she knows, how to use it. The other one's quieter. Used to being pushed aside, I think, and before I can stop it, I feel myself smile because they'll find out; sooner or later they'll find out how wrong they've been. She's got something the little one'll never have and it's foolish of them to ignore it.

The woman in orange is staring at me. She must have seen my smile. I make myself sit up very straight and fold my hands together in my lap.

'Miranda? That's right, isn't it? Miranda.'

'Yes.'

'I haven't met you before, have I? This your first time here?'

'Not exactly.' Then, because that's what we'd decided, I add, 'I'm a friend of James,' and Leonardo's right, she's immediately disconcerted.

'James?' She makes a little moue of disdain. 'Oh! James!'

I smile. 'Oh, there's more to James than the obvious,' and I almost laugh then, because she doesn't like it, me having inside knowledge about someone she's known most of her life.

'I am the children's aunt,' she says. 'Jackie…' She pauses to put down her glass. 'Jackie is my sister.'

I nod. I can't think of anything to say. I wish Leonardo had listened to me; I don't want to be here; whatever he says, these are not my kind of people.

'Perhaps,' she says, leaning toward me with something like a smile, 'perhaps we could go for a walk.'

Earlier, I'd kicked off my shoes. They're hidden somewhere under the couch. To bend down to retrieve them I'd look like a child…gauche. I get up and follow her in my stockinged feet and she doesn't notice, not even when we cross the terrace and I stumble a little on the gravelled path.

'The roses…they've almost finished but they're still…' I begin but she merely shrugs and I don't try again.

She indicates a bench under the liquidambar. 'We'll sit there,' and after a few moments, she says, 'I got my mother out of that home they'd put her in. I couldn't leave her there.' She stops and adds in quite a different voice, 'She used to beat me, you know.'

'Then why…?'

Her eyes search my face. I swallow and look away. The sunlit garden, James, Leonardo, even the children, they're nothing, they haven't happened yet, they're still all in the future. I'm a little girl, cowering, and my mother is coming towards me with mad eyes, my father's belt twitching in her hands.

'You…you must be an extraordinary person,' I whisper. 'I'd have left her there.'

'I couldn't do that. She was my mother.' She sighs and smoothes her dress over her knees. 'And now poor Claude and the children. I'll have to do something about them.'

'But what about Jackie? Surely Jackie…'

She laughs. 'You can't depend on Jackie.' She bends down and picks up a leaf from the grass. It's shaped like a star and trembles for a moment in her hand as if it's reluctant to give up being alive. 'Poor Claude,' she says. 'If he hadn't had the accident... Well, even then, Jackie... She was tiring of him. I could see it, I've always been able to see it when she's getting ready to move on. And the children... I could never understand why she had them. Of course a son, obviously Claude wanted a son, but even so...' She pauses again and puts the leaf down on the bench next to her. 'Poor Claude. He never had a chance. Sometimes I think...well, no doubt it's wicked of me but I'm glad he had the accident because otherwise, otherwise he'd have found out what she is and I don't think he would have been able to bear it.' She's quiet then, staring off into the distance, blue hills and even bluer sky.

'You love him,' I whisper. 'You love Claude.'

'Yes.' She smiles but it's not for me, her smile, it's for someone else, herself perhaps, the young girl she'd been, watching her little sister flaunting herself with her mother's guests. 'How...how did you know?'

I don't tell her. How can I? I love Leonardo and he...he...

'Watching,' I say. 'All my life I've been watching and so...' I put my hand out and lay it on her arm. I make my voice steady. I have to. I have to out of respect for the careful way she's holding herself still. 'I know. That's what matters. I know. Someone else knows.'

'Yes,' she whispers. 'Yes.'

The light on her bent head's suddenly kind. It gives her face an unexpected gentleness before it shifts and finds the bright colour of her dress.

Oak

They're shouting again. I lie very still and concentrate on willing them to stop. Brittany says thoughts have power. Her chin jutted out when she said it and she looked fierce. I hope she's right. Once Mum and Dave start, it's usually hours before they stop.

Jarrod begins to whimper. They've woken him up. I clench my hands under the blankets. Jarrod's crying will only make them worse. 'Shut that bloody kid up,' Dave'll shout. 'What sort of mother are you when you can't even keep him from bawling?' It isn't fair. It's not all Mum's fault.

I get out of bed. I'm frightened of Dave. He doesn't like me. But Jarrod's crying so I've got to get him. I don't want Dave to hit him again. Or Mum. When they're angry, they forget he's just a baby.

I creep into his room. It's dark but I can see all right because of the street light outside. Jarrod's standing up, hanging onto the bars of his cot. It's something he's just learned to do. I haul him out. 'Ssh,' I whisper. 'You're safe now.' I feel better holding him. Strong. It's a good feeling. I'm not frightened any more. Jarrod loves me.

Brittany says he loves me most. She doesn't say it spitefully, though. She isn't like that. Anyway, she's got Megan. 'A sister for me, a brother for you,' she said when Jarrod was born last year. I laughed. She made it sound like a maths problem.

'All the same,' I whisper to Jarrod as I put him in bed next to me, 'all the same, she's right. You an' me, Jarrod, we're brothers and that means I have to look out for you.'

Jarrod puts his fingers in his mouth and starts to slurp on them. I cuddle up to him.

After a while, I don't hear Mum and Dave any more, only Jarrod slurping.

Brittany wakes me up. It's still so early the light's all yellow round the edge of the blind and you can't see the furniture properly. I turn over but Brittany keeps poking me.

'Jamie,' she hisses. 'Come on. Wake up. I've got something to tell you.'

'What?' I sit up and push the hair out of my eyes.

Jarrod's asleep next to me. His hair's all tousled into curls and he's got his arms flung up over his head. I tuck the blanket round him so he won't get cold and turn to Brittany.

'What is it? What's wrong?'

Brittany makes herself comfortable on the end of my bed. She hunches her knees and rests her chin on them. 'Dave's gone,' she says. She tries to keep her face under control but she can't help herself. It breaks up into a smile.

I let my breath out. 'How do you know?' I whisper.

'Heard him. Wonder you didn't. Last night. They were going on at one another and then he shouted "I've had enough" and the front door slammed so I reckon that's it. He's gone.'

'But he might come back... I mean...'

'Don't think so. It sounded pretty final to me. Mum didn't run after him either, not like she usually does.'

I don't know what to say. Brittany's all lit up like it's Christmas. She doesn't like Dave any more than I do.

''Course you never know with Mum. She'll probably get someone else. Might even be worse than Dave.'

'Don't say that. I'd rather Dave back than that. Anyway, he might...'

Brittany's face goes fierce. 'Don't be stupid. He won't come back. Once they've gone, they've gone. You ought to know that. Look at our father.'

I nod. Our father left a long time ago. We haven't heard from him since. I go inside myself trying to remember. His hands. Our father had large, square hands. 'He liked to fix things,' I whisper. 'And once...once he held me up and showed me the stars. He said they all had names...'

My voice trails away but Brittany doesn't answer. Her face is all shut up. She won't ever talk about our father. I wish she would. She's older than me. She could tell me things I've forgotten. Together we could make him real.

Suddenly Brittany jumps up. 'I'm going to make us a special breakfast to celebrate. Pancakes. You want pancakes, Jamie? I'm sure there's some milk and eggs left.'

'All right.'

Brittany's big on breakfast. It's one of her things. Don't ask me why. I never feel much like eating in the mornings.

I snuggle down next to Jarrod for a few more minutes. It's still early. I'm not too sure about Dave leaving. I'm glad of course but… I don't like things changing. I like to know what's going to happen next. Even bad things. If you know about them, you can plan what to do. You're prepared.

Dave's been with Mum a long time. Nearly two years. He's Jarrod's father. He makes a big thing of it. 'My son,' he'll say and his eyes'll go all fierce and proud like it's something special. It makes me feel bad. I'm glad for Jarrod of course but my father never felt like that about me, otherwise he…

I bite at my lip and look at my brother. 'It's all right, Jarrod,' I tell him. 'Fathers don't matter.'

I want to cry then. I don't know why. I'm glad he's gone but I still feel like crying.

*

I'm late home from school.

Brittany's at the kitchen table, frowning over her homework. 'Where have you been? Jarrod's been grizzling for the last hour. I couldn't get him out. I've got this to finish.'

I sigh and put down my backpack. 'Where's Mum?'

'She's taken Megan to the doctor. Her ear's bad again. She had to get her from school. They rang up.'

I start towards the door but Brittany stops me. 'Jamie, wait up. We… we have to move again.'

'But we've only just got here. I mean…' My voice rises. 'You said, you promised, Brittany, that we'd stay here at least six months. You said there was a, a lease and it…'

'Yes, I know and I thought…' She takes a deep breath and begins again. 'I'm sorry, Jamie. It's because of Dave, him leaving. Mum can't

27

afford the rent. Not without him. I asked her where we'd go but she doesn't know. She just burst into tears and then…'

'Brittany.' I take a step towards her. 'Brittany, she won't, she won't put us in foster care again, will she? I mean, last time she…'

'No, of course not. She was sick then. Depressed. That's what they said, depressed, and…' She stops suddenly. Her eyes flinch away from mine.

I grip the back of a chair and swallow hard. Brittany's scared, she's just as scared as me. She's trying to hide it but I can tell. I look away quickly. The clock. The clock on the shelf above the refrigerator. I focus on that.

Brittany gets up and starts putting her books in her bag. 'Get Jarrod,' she says at last. 'He probably needs his bottle. You see to him and I'll…I'll start on tea. We'll have everything ready when Mum gets home, everything nice. She'll be pleased. You get Jarrod and play with him so he'll be tired and go to bed early.' Brittany lifts her chin. 'We'll show her how good it can be without Dave. It'll be all right. I promise, Jamie, I promise I won't let her send us all away again.'

I nod. She's doing it for me. Reassuring me. It isn't fair. She shouldn't have to. I open my mouth but the feelings inside me are all jumbled up and I don't know how to tell her. I turn and run into Jarrod's room.

*

Mum backs the car up the driveway. It's hard to tell what the house is like because it's all overgrown with some sort of creeper.

Brittany turns round to look at me. 'It's not too bad, is it?' she whispers.

Mum slams on the brakes and fumbles with the door handle. 'Come on, you two,' she says. 'Hurry up and get the stuff out the back. I haven't got all day.'

Brittany doesn't say anything; she's out of the car almost as quickly as Mum.

I clamber slowly over a pile of boxes on the back seat. I pause to get a better look at the house. I move a bit closer and squint up my eyes. It looks good then. A blur of green and grey and the blue, blue sky. 'I don't really care what you're like,' I whisper. 'Just, just as long as we can stay here a long, long time.' I cross my fingers and hide them behind my back. That's meant to work. That's meant to make wishes come true.

'Jamie,' yells Brittany. 'Come on.' She dumps a pile of blankets in my arms. 'Mum wants us to take everything inside while she goes back for Megan and Jarrod. Auntie Linda's got to go to work at ten.'

I follow Brittany across the lawn and up the front steps.

'Careful,' warns Brittany. 'They're a bit wonky. Uncle Brian's going to fix them.' She unlocks the front door.

Uncle Brian brought most of our stuff over last night in his trailer so the lounge looks almost familiar. Mum's chair. The sagging davenport. The television. The wilting rubber plant Dave gave Mum for her last birthday. I let the blankets slide to the floor.

''S all right, isn't it?' says Brittany. 'Come on. There's heaps of boxes. You wanna get yours and put them in your room while I start on the kitchen.'

'Okay.'

Brittany came over last night with Uncle Brian so she knows where everything is. She takes me to show me my room. It's right at the back of the house. She flicks on the light switch and I take a step forward but then I stop.

'I…I can't sleep here, Brittany. There isn't any light. I mean, look, the window's boarded up.'

'Mum said the landlord's promised to fix it.'

I clutch at her arm. 'They never do what they say. You know they don't. Even Uncle Brian. It's just…just promises and… Oh, Brittany, I can't stay here. I can't. It's like…it's like a prison cell.'

Brittany ducks her head. 'I know it's awful. I told Mum. I told her I'd have it instead but she said it's too small for me and Megan. Oh, Jamie, I…' She hesitates and when I don't say anything, she bites at her lips and adds, 'I'll let you have my whale poster if you like. We could put it on the wall there. Hey, you could pretend you were underwater. Maybe Mum would let us get some blue paint and we could…'

I pull at the frayed edge of my T-shirt.

Brittany's voice rises. 'You know what I reckon we ought to do? A mural. Textas would be good enough for that. Hey, how about a wall each and we'll draw fish and crabs and things. 'Course Jarrod can't but the rest of us.' She throws me a quick look. 'Megan can draw all right.'

I know what she means. Ever since Megan started school six months ago, there's been trouble about her. Mum keeps getting letters from the teachers. A special needs child. That's what they keep saying. Brittany had to read the last letter out loud because Mum's not too good at reading. ''S all right,' Brittany told Mum when she'd finished. 'She's special and we need her.' Mum smiled then. She knew it wasn't what they meant, we all did, but somehow Brittany had made it all right again. And Megan *is* special. You just have to look at her to see that. She's got all this fair hair, curls like you see in old-fashioned pictures, and a little pointed face and really dark eyes. You'd think that'd be enough, the way she looks; you wouldn't think they'd expect anything more.

I start to feel a bit better. 'Yeah,' I say slowly. 'Yeah.' I start to plan out my wall. A coral reef perhaps, with sea horses and little darting fish. Yes, and among the rocks I'll do some of those sea flowers – anemones, that's what they're called – and...

All afternoon we help Mum unpack. She's in one of her moods. I can tell by the way her lips are pursed together. We are all careful not to annoy her but then Jarrod wakes up. He's in his cot in the lounge; there isn't room anywhere else.

When she hears him, Mum's head jerks up. 'Get him, Jamie. Take him outside. I can't put up with his whingeing, not with my head aching the way it is.'

I haul him out and carry him into the kitchen. 'He's awfully wet, Mum. Don't you think...'

'I said, take him outside. You going deaf or something?' She takes a step towards me, her hand raised.

Brittany grabs hold of Megan. 'We'll all go outside for a while,' she says quickly. 'You have a bit of a rest, Mum.'

Mum sinks down in the nearest chair. 'Yeah, all right.'

The danger's over. I flash Brittany a grateful glance and follow her and Megan outside. There's a bit of a veranda, some more steps. Jarrod's heavy and I watch my feet so I won't fall. I hear Brittany catch her breath and then stop.

'Jamie. Jamie, look. Look at the tree.'

It fills the backyard. I've never seen anything like it. So big and... I rush over to it and stare up at the sky through a canopy of quivering, dark green leaves. The light wavers in patterns on the ground. I can feel it on my face too. Warm. It reaches inside me and I shake my head in wonder. It's like when you're having a bad dream and you wake up and it's morning and you know for sure that the dream isn't real.

Brittany turns to me with shining eyes. She looks different. Like Megan. Like Megan when she's found something she likes, a bit of silver paper or a bird's feather. We all feel the same. I know we do. I smile at Brittany and look around for Megan. She's sitting on the grass, a leaf in her hands; she's carefully turning it round and round and crooning to it.

I shift Jarrod onto my other hip. 'Look,' I whisper. 'Look, Jarrod. Tree.'

'It's an oak,' says Brittany, squinting up her eyes. 'I'm sure it's an oak. I've seen pictures of them in library books.'

I put Jarrod down next to Megan. Then I step forward. 'Hello, Oak,' I say boldly. 'I'm Jamie and these are my sisters, Brittany and Megan, and my baby brother Jarrod…'

*

I've never thought much about trees. I mean, they're just there. Apple, almond, apricot. Spring, of course, I've noticed them then, all sort of lacy and there're always gum trees in the park, their leaves hanging and changing colour in the wind. I tried to draw them once but I didn't have the right colours. There's only two greens in a box of coloured pencils and they're both too bright. Dave found me with it and roared with laughter. 'Hey, look at this, Raelene,' he shouted, waving my picture at Mum. 'Kid thinks he's an artist. Drawing leaves. Leaves, for crying out loud. What d'ye reckon? Must be some kind of little pouf.'

I clench my hands. Then I make myself take a deep breath. Dave's gone. It doesn't matter what he said. I can feel Oak behind me. His trunk. It's reassuring. 'I could draw your leaves all right,' I say slowly. 'They'd be difficult, all those curvy bits but they'd look good.' I nod. 'Oak,' I add solemnly. 'You've got distinctive leaves.' I lean back against him and close my eyes. I start planning out a picture. It's different from when we did my walls. That was all of us. This is just me. It's months since I did a picture just for myself.

31

*

I don't mind my room so much now. In the evenings, when Brittany's busy with her homework, I take Jarrod and Megan in there and we play with the blocks Jarrod got for his birthday.

'Let's build a house for the red people,' I say.

I pile up all the red blocks till, laughing, Jarrod leans forward and knocks them over.

Megan looks solemn. 'What'll happen to the red people now?' she whispers. 'Jamie, where'll the red people go now?'

'Oh, you don't have to worry about them,' I say. 'They'll just move in with the rainbow people. No matter what colour you are, you can live with the rainbow people.'

Megan smiles and reaches for a handful of blocks. 'I'll build their house then,' she says. 'I'll make it really big.'

I hold Jarrod on my lap. 'That's Megan's house,' I say. 'That's for the rainbow people. You can't knock that one down.'

Jarrod wriggles and tries to get away so I distract him by showing him how to bang two blocks together.

*

Every day, after school, I go into the backyard and talk to Oak. I like talking to him. He listens to everything I say. Most people don't. Or, if they do, they laugh. But it's different with Oak. I'm safe with him.

'I was wrong about trees, wasn't I, Oak?' I whisper. 'I thought they weren't important.'

I fling myself down on the grass next to him and let the sunlight prickle against my closed eyelids, the same sunlight that Oak can feel on his leaves.

'I reckon trees are just like people,' I tell him. 'We need the same things. Light and warmth and…and love. You need love too, don't you, Oak?'

I sit up and hug my knees. I love Brittany and Megan and Jarrod. I frown then and scrabble in the dirt with one hand. Mum. There's Mum too and Dad. I shake my head. It's hard loving people. They do things you don't understand, they leave and… I bite down hard on my lip. But Oak's different. I can feel him behind me. Steady. Oak's steady. You can trust him. My eyes sting with tears and I wipe them with my sleeve.

'I love you, Oak,' I whisper.

It's very quiet. A car in the street. A dog barking. The wind sighing in Oak's leaves. I look around me in wonder. The quietness is inside me. I like it. I want it to stay for always.

*

Megan pushes open my door. 'Look, Jamie,' she says. 'Look what I did at school.' She's got some pieces of paper in her hand. They're coloured all over in crayon; red and green and purple. She starts to lay them out carefully on my bed. 'They're bark rubbings,' she says, nodding importantly. 'The teacher said. She took us outside and showed us how to do them.'

I frown. She's right. You can see faint patterns in the colour. I hold one up to the light. It has a fairy-like look to it. 'They're good,' I say.

Megan picks one up. 'This is Oak,' she says. 'I made it for you when I got home.'

I take it from her. It doesn't really look any different from the others but I can tell Megan thinks it's special.

'Purple,' I say. 'I'm glad you made Oak purple.' I remember something I read somewhere. 'Purple's the colour of kings.'

Megan's stopped listening, though. She's re-arranging the pictures on my bed. Her lips are moving but I can't hear what she's saying.

Very gently, I lay the picture of Oak on my pillow and get on with writing out my spelling words.

*

Oak's changing me. I know he is. I can feel it. Like kids teasing me. I don't listen any more. I think about him instead.

I'm making a list of tree words. When I've got a lot, I'm going to make a poem. I found a new one today. Fortitude. It's sort of like strong but better.

'I'm going to have fortitude too,' I tell him. 'I'm going to be just like you.'

*

I take Jarrod outside to play. He isn't a baby now. He can walk. I lean against Oak and watch him stagger across the grass after his ball. He sits down suddenly in the middle of the lawn and looks around him, astonished. When his face begins to pucker, I rush over and grab him. I lift him as high as I can.

'Look at Oak's leaves,' I say. 'Look at them dancing in the light.'

Jarrod laughs then and reaches out his hands. I whirl him round and round until we're both dizzy. The light dances with us. It's like Oak's smiling, like the light is part of Oak.

I put Jarrod down and sink down next to him. 'It's good here, isn't it, Jarrod,' I say. 'It's good here with Oak.'

Jarrod looks solemn. Then he puts his fingers in his mouth and begins to slurp on them.

*

I wake up. It's dark. In the room next to mine, I can hear Megan singing. Her voice is high and very sweet, like birdsong, I think and then I don't think any more, I just listen. Megan's singing isn't like anything I've ever heard. It gets inside you and makes you want to cry.

Megan hasn't sung for months, not since she started school. I smile into the darkness. It's because of Oak. I know it is. Megan feels about Oak just like I do. He's made her feel safe again.

*

The sky's changed. It's just as blue but it's different. I tip my head back and screw up my eyes, frowning. Round the side of the house, the grass is stiff with frost. My hands are so cold I put them in my pockets and hunch down in my windcheater. It's all right, though. By recess, it'll be hot again. I walk to school slowly. I wish I knew how to draw frost. A whole page of grass, I think, each blade separate and outlined in silver. Maybe a fence too, a wire one hung with spider webs…

*

Megan and I chase Jarrod around the garden till he screams with laughter. Suddenly Megan stops. She puts her hand out and touches Oak's trunk. Her face goes still. I recognise the look. She's gone inside herself. She's listening, listening to music that no one else can hear. I pick up Jarrod and take him inside. Megan's forgotten about us but I don't mind. I'm glad she's happy again.

*

There's a scatter of leaves under Oak. I stare at them. Jarrod picks one up. It's brown instead of green. I walk right up to Oak. There's a sigh of wind and another leaf flutters down. Jarrod reaches for it, laughing. Two more. The wind catches them and whirls them round.

I snatch Jarrod up. 'Brittany, Brittany.' I run inside and dump Jarrod in his cot. 'Brittany, come quick. There's something wrong with Oak's leaves. They're dying. Oh, Brittany, what can we do? Oak is dying.'

Brittany's in her room. She looks up from the map she's drawing. She doesn't laugh but her lips twitch suspiciously. 'It's autumn, you idiot. Oak trees come from England. You know that. They're deciduous.'

'Decid–?' Then I remember. I'm embarrassed. 'Oh, of course. I'm, I'm stupid, aren't I?'

Brittany's mouth twists again. Then she puts down her pencil. I don't like the way she looks at me. 'Jamie,' she says slowly. 'Jamie, there's something I've got to tell you. I thought I'd wait a bit but maybe it's best if you know now so you'll have time to get used to it.'

'What?' I start re-arranging her pencils. I put the colours I like in front. Green. Green's my favourite, the colour of grass and leaves, green the colour of life and blue for the sky and purple for the shadows, yes the shadows under Oak in the evenings and yellow for sunshine…

'We're moving. In three weeks. Mum's going back to Dave. They…'

My head jerks up. 'No.' I grip the edge of the table with both hands.

35

'No.' I'm shaking. In a violent storm, Oak'd shake like this, all his branches and his leaves. I try to square my shoulders because Oak stands firm no matter what but I'm a boy, only a boy and… 'We can't,' I whisper. 'Oh, Brittany, we can't. I, I can't leave Oak. …'

Brittany reaches out and puts her hand on my arm. Her eyes are wide and dark and they look beyond me. She lifts her chin. 'It'll be all right. I'm going to make it all right. Just as soon as I'm old enough, I'm going to get a job, a good job that pays a lot and I'll get a place for us, a place where we can stay for always, all of us, you and me and Megan and Jarrod and we'll be happy. I promise, Jamie, I promise.'

Her face is fierce but her hands, her hands clutch at the edge of her desk and I know…I know…

My mouth is so dry I can barely whisper. 'No. It'll be too late then. You know it will.' Then I stop. I can't go on. But it doesn't matter. Nothing matters. Not any more. I turn and stumble to my room.

*

I try to talk to Oak. I don't think he can hear me, though. Most of his leaves have gone. The few that are left are brown and tattered. Ugly. I stare up through his bare branches at the overcast sky. I put my hand on his trunk. It's empty. Oak isn't in it any more.

'You're just a skeleton, Oak,' I tell him. 'I know how you feel. It's such a long time till spring. Brittany says you'll grow new leaves then. I'd have liked to have seen them but oh, Oak, I won't be here when you come back.' I start to sob then. I can't help it. 'Fortitude,' I whisper, choking. 'Fortitude.' It isn't enough. Patience. Strength. Even courage. None of them are enough.

*

We pack up again.

Dave comes to help. He's grinning all over his face. He tousles my hair. 'Hey, Jamie,' he says. 'You miss me?' Then he laughs.

I don't say anything. I don't even try to pull away.

Dave shrugs and goes off to help Mum and Brittany with the chest of drawers.

*

Dave's got a place not far from where we used to live. I don't care. I don't care about anything.

*

I do what they want. I go to school. I take Jarrod and Megan for long walks in the park. I listen to Brittany's plans for the future. But it's like it's not happening. Not to me. It's like I'm just watching.

Once or twice, I get frightened. I can feel myself disappearing. I try to talk to Oak in my mind but he's gone. We've both gone and I don't know how to get either of us back.

After a while, I don't even want to.

*

I'm in my room. I go inside myself to the darkness I like.

The door opens. It's Brittany and Megan. I frown. They're interrupting. I don't move. I wait for them to leave. They always do. They don't like my silences. I think they're frightened of them.

Brittany comes right up to my bed. 'Jamie,' she says.

Her voice is so loud, I flinch and put my arms over my face.

'Jamie,' she says again. She reaches over and grabs me by the shoulder. 'Jamie, listen. Megan's got something for you.'

I feel my breath shudder in my chest and I open my eyes and sit up. I try to see what Megan's got in her hand. It's brown and smooth and shiny. I feel myself frown.

'It's an acorn,' she whispers. 'Brittany says if you plant it, you can grow your own oak tree.'

My mouth is suddenly dry. I turn to Brittany. She's watching me, her lips pursed, her eyes wary. I feel my throat get tight. I don't want to say anything but Brittany's face, her eyes and…and… I stare at the acorn in Megan's hand. Her hand is so small. It's curled around the acorn, protecting it.

'Brittany,' I whisper at last. 'Brittany.' I swallow hard. 'Tomorrow,' I say slowly. 'Tomorrow we'll find an old tin and some dirt and…'

Megan bends forward and, very carefully, tips the acorn into my cupped hands. I look at it for a long time in silence. Then I lift my head.

'It's throbbing. Megan, I can feel the life in it throbbing. You wouldn't think so, would you? You wouldn't think you could but it's alive. It's alive.'

Megan's eyes go suddenly wide with wonder.

'I told you,' Brittany says smiling and nodding at her. 'I told you, Megan, didn't I? I told you Jamie'd know it was special. After all, it's got part of Oak inside it.'

Brittany turns to me then and touches the acorn with one finger. 'Jamie,' she says. 'Jamie, it's almost spring. A few more days and...'

I nod. I close my eyes. I can feel it. Spring. Oak's leaves are beginning to unfurl. I know they are. My heart lurches. The light on them is so tender. I can feel it, little reaching fingers of light...

'Let's not wait till tomorrow,' I say, jumping up. 'Come on. Let's get a tin and plant Acorn now.'

Megan laughs. She catches hold of my hand and pulls me to the door and we all go outside together.

The Morning After

As soon as they tell her she can get up, Sinead makes her way down the corridor to the communal bathroom. She wants to see if her face has changed. She's heard it so often, her high school friend Layla, the woman at the boarding house where they'd spent their honeymoon, Kurt himself, laughing, 'You look like a child.' And she knows they're right. She's seen it for herself. There's something soft and unformed in her face. Her clothes, too, they never seem to fit properly. Her mother twitching impatiently at her collar, the band of her skirt, 'You need to take some pride in your appearance. You're grown up now,' though for years and years, ever since she joined the church, she's been saying, her mouth prim and pious, 'Pride, the sin by which the angels fell,' and Sinead has wanted, oh! so often, to remind her but she's never quite dared because her mother might say she's grown up but she's never treated her as if she is. Not even now. Not even now when…

'I'm not a child,' she whispers and her head jerks up and she's fierce and determined. 'After last night, I can't ever be a child again,' and she smiles, suddenly confident.

She pushes open the door marked 'Bathroom' and steps inside. It's smaller than she expected, narrow, a glimpse of sky through a half-open window, cream walls, tiles and, above a single basin, a severe, square mirror.

It hasn't changed. Her face, there in front of her. It hasn't changed at all. She puts her hand out tentatively and the girl in the mirror responds, smiling, her mouth still sweet, still too tender and her eyes… Surely, though, her eyes are different, shadowed perhaps and her hair, her long, tangled, Alice-in-Wonderland hair… 'Bedraggled,' whispers Sinead and she takes comfort from it because at least it's something tangible, something later she can tell herself.

Sighing, she goes into the stall to use the toilet there. Her movements are slow, awkward. It's as if her body isn't hers, not yet, and maybe it won't ever… She wants her face to be different but not her body. 'The same,' she whispers, clenching her hands. 'I want it to go back to being the same as before.'

The other women in the ward, they talk casually about getting their figures back, pelvic floor contractions, and she's listened but she hasn't said anything because she's seen it in their faces, they think she's a child too, she shouldn't be there with them, she should be back at school frowning over algebra and Dylan Thomas and Europe after Waterloo.

She stands up again, sighing. It used to be so simple. She was a little girl running in the rain, clambering over rocks at the beach, pumping herself higher and higher on her swing and she didn't know…how could she… Pain…she didn't know anything about pain. She'd thought she did. A scraped knee. Fever. A septic throat. What was that? What was any of that when last night…

She shudders, remembering and hears again her voice, shouting, 'I don't know what's happening to me'…and all the time she knows, of course she knows…her mind tells her but her body, her body's no longer connected to her mind, it's doing what it has to and she, she's no longer in control.

The midwife leans over to push the damp hair out of her eyes. Her uniform's stained with blood. It frightens her, the blood…all the books she'd read, they never said anything about blood…Braxton-Hicks…the three stages of labour…but they never said anything about blood or she'd have remembered…

'The…the blood…' she whispers. 'Where…where did the blood…?'

But the midwife shakes her head and says, wearily, 'Stop fighting it. Otherwise we'll both be here all night. Go with it. Go with the pain,' and she holds the mask over her face, though Sinead, protesting, tries to push it away.

'I can't breathe.'

'Don't be ridiculous. It'll help you.'

Then…it's over…so sudden…a baby crying… The sound of it fills the room, fills the place where the pain had been…

She'd watched her hands reach out…eager…pleading…but after a brief moment, my baby, oh! my baby, they'd taken her away. She'd sunk back on the pillows. Nothing…all those hours but nothing as bad as this, watching them wheel her baby away in a little plastic cot…her baby crying, a shock of dark hair and little flailing fists…

'Please…'

'Later. In the morning. You can see her then.'

'But I…'

'All in good time, dear. We have to weigh her, dress her.' Then, suddenly, putting her hand on Sinead's arm as if….as if the long night hadn't happened, the long night when they'd been combatants on different sides, 'You've got a lovely little girl, dear. She'll be with you soon enough.'

Sinead, in front of the mirror, washing her face with her cupped hands, lifts her head again. 'So you ought to look different. You ought to look…' She stops mid-sentence. She's remembering holding the baby for the first time.

Everything. Everything that's been important in her life. Spring blossom. A falling star. Kurt telling her he loved her. The light on her wedding veil when she stepped out of the car to go into the church. The smell of frangipani. None of that significant. Not now. Not now she's held her, her own baby.

She hardly hears the door slam behind her. She's hurrying back along the corridor to her room. The baby's in a cot by the bed and she can't bear to be separated from her any longer.

White Bird

When I caught the bus this morning, the sky was different. It was wide and blue and somehow tender. Now there are clouds along the horizon, thin and teased out, the mares' tails they told us about at school. Above them, where the sun's dipping, something else, the beginning of a dark bruising. I look quickly away.

'Cranesbill's next,' says the bus driver without turning. 'That's the stop you wanted, isn't it, love?'

'Yes.'

Between the round bales of hay, stubble, but along the fence, stiff as sentinels, speared grass and a tangle of blood-red pincushion flowers. I put my hand out and start to trace their shapes on the windowpane.

The bus is slowing down. The town's a collection of weatherboard cottages…a wooden bench outside a general store…scribbled gums…a blue heeler dog stretched out, panting, on the pub veranda. The bus jerks to a stop in front of a corrugated iron shelter and I grab up my backpack and stumble down the aisle.

'That all your luggage?'

'Yes.' I hesitate. 'Thank you.'

He smiles then and I'm a little girl again, pigtails flying, jumping down from the school bus.

I pull myself back to the present and drop my bag at my feet. Coming towards me, a woman. Brisk. Purposeful. Navy skirt and a wide-brimmed linen hat. My mother's Aunt Margaret.

'Cara? It is you, isn't it? You've grown so, I hardly recognised you but never mind, we can get to know one another all over again.' My body's stiff in her arms and she's pressing her cheek against mine. 'Oh, Cara, it is so good to see you. Such a surprise, such a lovely surprise when your mother rang.' She pushes me away and her eyes go over my face as if she's

42

looking for something.

I duck my head. My hands have laced themselves through the straps of my bag. White on black. A kind of pattern.

Auntie Margaret's suddenly not sure of herself, I can feel it, but she goes on steadily, 'Come along then. I've got our supper all ready. Nothing elaborate, just cold chicken and salad. Christine tells me you've been sick.'

'No.' The truth. For once, no matter what, the truth. 'I had an abortion.'

'Oh, my dear.' It's no more than a whisper but it's enough. She's not like my mother.

We go on in silence. The church. The deserted schoolyard. A paddock of running horses. Flying manes and tails and, under the trees with his mother, a little staggering foal outlined in a fuzz of gold. Then the cottage. A pink-flowered tree. An uneven brick path. The green front door.

'Here we are,' and we're down a step and inside.

The light's dull. Smoked glass, I think, though, really, the windows are ordinary enough – small, though – with little diamond bits that cut them into patterns. A crimson rug. A grey sofa. A vase of sweet-peas on a little round table. On a stand in the corner, a white bird in a large square cage.

I run over to it and poke my fingers through the bars. 'Oh. Oh, Auntie Margaret.'

'That's Harry.' She's in the adjoining kitchen now, setting plates out on a pine table. 'He's a canary. In the morning, you'll hear him sing.'

'But...but aren't canaries yellow?'

'Not always. Bit like us. They're all different.'

I hear her go to the stove and light the gas jet under the kettle.

'Now, do you want to eat first or would you rather I show you round?'

'I don't care. Eat, I suppose.'

Harry smoothes his feathers with his beak and pauses, head on one side, to watch me.

'How can he sing when he's shut up in a cage?'

'Oh, Cara, love, he doesn't know any different. He's been bred to it.'

'That's worse. That's...'

'No.' She comes back and puts her arm around me. 'You think about it. He's safe here with me. Nothing can hurt him. Outside... if I let him out, he'd have all sorts of things to contend with...'

43

'He'd be free.'

'None of us are free. The wild birds, watch them for a while and you'll see they aren't free either. Not really. Danger…it's all around them and they know…'

I jerk myself away. 'If you say so.'

'Cara…'

I grab up my bag and hold it against my chest. 'I'm tired,' I shout. 'I don't want anything to eat. I want to go to my room.' My mouth quivers despite myself. 'You do have a room for me, don't you?'

'Of course I have. Your mother….' She doesn't finish. Her cheeks go pink and she says quickly, 'Come along then, dear. I hope…I just hope… Well, anything you want – anything at all – you just have to ask.'

I feel bad then. It isn't her fault. I know that. It isn't my mother's either. Or Justin's. It's mine. I let them do it to me. I didn't make any sort of protest at all.

*

The room's all right. It's out the back, part of an enclosed veranda, with narrow, louvred windows and cement-rendered walls. I slide my fingers along them. I like the feel of them. Then I look around. There's a camp bed with a striped yellow quilt, a chair, a wooden cupboard. I drop my bag on the floor and fling myself face down on the bed. I don't cry, though. I've promised myself, I'm never going to cry again.

After a while, I sit up. It's got dark. I feel myself start to smile. The dark's safe. It hides things. And the things it doesn't hide, it changes so you can't recognise them.

The house is very quiet. Auntie Margaret must have gone to bed because I can't hear her. Outside, it's different. A bird. A dog barking. Somewhere, a long way off, a car…

I swing my legs over the side of the bed and go across to the door to turn on the light. Nights like this when I can't sleep, I draw. Sometimes it's good. I make up other worlds. Forests of dancing trees. An underwater garden. A pool with water lily swans. Other times… I bite at my lip and grab up my backpack. My sketchbook's there and the graphite pencils I stole from the art room at school. I turn the book upside down so I can start at the back.

I don't want to see the pictures I've done of the baby. They frighten me. I'd be seven months gone by now and he'd look real. Ears and eyes and little outstretched hands.

Frowning, I start to draw. Clouds. A twist of barbed wire. A fallen gum tree. Harry. None of them look right. In desperation, I draw the baby's hands again. I can't help it. It's all I can see...his little hands... reaching...reaching...

*

Morning. Patterns of light on the tiled floor. I get up and go into the kitchen where Auntie Margaret's making us breakfast. Boiled eggs. Toast. Coffee.

'Did you sleep well?'

I nod and sit down. I'm never much good in the mornings. It's all right, though, because it looks like she's the same.

When I've finished eating, I take my coffee into the next room so I can drink it in front of Harry's cage. 'I heard him sing.'

Auntie Margaret comes over to join me. 'Yes,' she says, smiling. 'I told you he didn't mind being in a cage.'

'Maybe.'

Harry jumps from one perch to another. He cocks his head at us. His eyes are bold and very black and they've got a shine to them. 'Polished,' I think, and for some reason it pleases me; it's like the line of a poem, the polish of his eyes, and I want suddenly to laugh because I've never understood poetry nor ever wanted to.

Harry's preening now, his wings, outstretched, quiver, his beak... I feel my breath catch in my throat. My mother at her tapestry and I, coming in from the library, my arms full of books.

'Mum. Mum, I've been reading and it said...' I stop and start again. 'When...when you were having me, Mum, what did it feel like? Me moving? Me moving for the first time inside you?'

'Oh, Cara.' Her face changing, going soft. 'Wings. It felt like the flutter of wings.' Then, suddenly, red-cheeked, shouting, 'Stop it. Stop it now. It wasn't a baby. It didn't have time to be a baby. Stop it, Cara. It was for the best. You know it was.'

I take my empty mug back into the kitchen and put it down by the sink. I pause a moment until my hands stop shaking and then I go into my room to get my sketch pad. I have to draw Harry. Properly. Without bars. 'Because …' I whisper fiercely. 'Because…' but I can't finish.

Feelings never work as words, only as pictures.

*

'Cara? Cara, love? You there?'

I get up from where I've been sitting by Harry's cage and carefully close my sketchbook.

Auntie Margaret's come in from the garden, her arms full of flowers. 'I have to go down to the shops to get us some milk. I thought…I thought you might like to come with me.' She puts the flowers on the table and starts arranging them in a vase. 'There's not much to see but we'd be going past the horses again and yesterday I thought…'

'I don't want…' I begin but then I lift my head and make my eyes meet hers. 'Tomorrow,' I say. 'I promise I'll come tomorrow.' I duck my head and watch my fingers trace circles on the table. 'I'm drawing Harry,' I whisper. 'I have to finish it.'

She hesitates. 'Maybe…maybe when you have, you'll show me. Only if you want to of course. I wouldn't…'

Her face is like a child's. It shows everything she feels. My face used to be like that. It isn't now. I've learned.

She finishes with the flowers and I watch her collect her things, hat, purse, string bag.

'I won't be long. You'll be all right by yourself, won't you? It's just for a few minutes but your mother said…'

'My mother's a liar,' and, tight-mouthed, I go back to my sketch pad and draw angry spirals till I'm myself again.

After a while, I throw down my pencil and sit, knees humped, watching Harry. 'You're never still,' I tell him and I remember the books I read in the library about the baby. He wouldn't have been still either. By now…

I jump up and push open the door to the cage. My hands, all by themselves, reach in and they know how to do it, they've got him, he's cupped between them, struggling and then, as I bring him out, he goes

46

suddenly quiet. 'Oh. Oh.' His eyes. His half-open beak. His tiny delicate-toed feet. 'Please,' I whisper, shutting my eyes. 'Please,' and I loosen my hold a little so I can feel him move again inside my hands.

He's free. All in a moment. He's confused, though. He stutters, almost falls, and I make a grab for him but I'm too late, he's turned, all at once confident, in front of him the kitchen and the window, wide and full of light.

He hits it. I hear myself cry out. I'm running forward and then I'm on my knees beside him. I pick him up. He's so small, smaller, oh! surely smaller than before, and the warm's still in him, the last of it but he, himself, has gone. 'Oh, Harry, Harry.' I'm crying now. He's cradled against my chest and I'm rocking us backwards and forwards. 'Oh, my baby, my baby.'

I'm still there when Auntie Margaret comes back.

'Cara, Cara, what is it?'

I thrust the dead bird at her and then, choking, I turn and run outside to my room, slamming the door behind me.

Green Silk

I keep thinking about you. I don't know why; I never have before. But now, waiting for the afternoon to turn into evening, I'm conscious of you watching me, frowning, from the shadows.

I've watched you too, of course. Not always willingly, perhaps, but I've dreamt I was you, hair across my face, running from the house where we spent our common childhood. I...or you...whichever one I am...I know what I want. A job. A place to live that's mine. A place I can be myself and not the person they want me to be. I'm sure I can find the answers in the newspaper advertisements, and it has to be my own newspaper, one I've bought yourself, not the one belonging to him, the man my mother says is my stepfather though really my mother isn't married to him. It's just another of her pretences. You didn't know that any more than I did, of course. Not then when we were young and desperate to know the truth. That's the trouble with being young. You think the truth's important. I'm sure, though, with what I know about you now, that you gave up believing in the truth long before I did.

I don't think, running through the streets, early morning with a pinkening sky behind you, I don't think you thought about me, that you'd be leaving me behind. Because that's when, I know it is, that's when we began our divided lives and there's no going back, no way we can ever be the same person again. We have chosen – you as well as me – to live in parallel universes.

I stayed on at home. I got a scholarship to university and then, after two years, trapped, dropped out to marry. I wish...the light across the floor is striped with shadow and it is too late for wishing but...I wish...I wish I had gone instead of you. I look around me quickly, the cat asleep on my bed, my pot plants in the kitchen window, the books piled by my chair, my things, all I've got left... I don't want them to hear...and you, I don't want you to hear either.

I saw you at the art gallery once. You were with a pale young man and you were both standing in front of the angel picture in the foyer. I wanted to run up to you and say, 'That's my picture. When I was at university I used to come in every day just to look at it. I pretended I was the angel. See, it's got a ball of light in its hands and it's smiling to itself because it's so proud to be asked to hold the light...'

I didn't, of course. I didn't think you'd understand. I wasn't her any more, the girl at university. I wasn't you either, not any more. We'd both changed too much.

I had the children with me, the baby in the pusher clutching his blankie, the older ones by my side. I whispered, 'Look, these are my children. At least I have them even if...even if...' but I wasn't sure if I was talking to you or the angel.

In any case, the angel had changed. Some of the wonder had gone out of its face. Perhaps it had realised it isn't a privilege to hold the light. Not really. You can't hide anything from the light and some things you need to hide. Like love. When it stops. You have to go on pretending... otherwise...the children... The children need a father and I...I...

The children. They've grown up. It's like they too happened to someone else. All I've got left are pictures, photographs crammed higgledy-piggledy in an old box on top of my wardrobe. I never look at them. I don't want to remember when they were little and I was important. I've regressed. It's like I'm running in the rain towards the railway station and I don't know if I'm you or you're me and the young woman, taut-mouthed, her crying baby held against her shoulder as she walks up and down in a darkened room is someone neither of us know at all.

I make myself get up and go over to the window. The evening light is so kind. I've always liked it. Against the iron fence there's a tangle of jasmine, pink-budded because it's spring again. I put my hand against the glass and watch my fingers draw the shape of the flowers. Tomorrow or the next day it will all be in flower...

Sometimes I pretend I visit you. You've got a place in the city, a balcony flat. I walk from room to room holding my breath. Black and white tiled kitchen. Bathroom with crimson towels. In an alcove, a stone statue of the Madonna. A blue and yellow jug. Above your bed, a little framed painting, a dead tree silhouetted against a striped sky. There are

49

bars on all the windows, not prison bars, another kind, elegantly curved as if they are there for beauty and not necessity.

You're on the balcony. I hesitate at the open French windows to watch you. You're leaning back in a wicker chair, one leg crossed over the other. Silk. You're dressed in green silk, though I'm not sure... I've never seen anyone dressed in silk, old-fashioned films perhaps, but... It falls around you, your dress, in elegant folds, the light on it is like light on water...mysterious...the sea... Your face is shaded with a white linen hat and you're drinking...a long-stemmed glass... Your hands don't look like mine...they're pale, slender, while my hands with their bitten nails are still the hands of a child.

You lift up your glass to look through it and I feel you smile. I start to shout, 'It isn't real. The world you're watching isn't real. You're seeing it through glass...' but then you half turn and I see your face and there's a sadness in it that makes me stop.

Something else. Something I remember. Your silk dress is the same colour as sea glass. Once – I was six, seven, still too young to know anything – the tide was coming in...a lace of foam and a piece of tumbled sea glass. I picked it up and looked through it just like you're looking through the liquid in your glass.

Beyond the balcony the wide sweep of the darkening city, the first lights coming on, little pinpricks like stars. You're sighing now. You let one finger trace around the rim of your glass. I know what you're doing. You're imagining you made different choices. You're imagining you're me. It's something I do all the time. Imagine I'm you.

The Lady Medea

I wake up and it's still night. Darkness. Wind. The spatter of rain against the open window. I get up to close it but then I start to shudder. I've remembered about *Medea*. We did it at high school. Euripides. After Jason left her, she took the sons she had borne him and killed them.

'No,' I whisper, 'no' and I let myself fall back on the bed. My room is suddenly full of shadows that clutch at one another and, frightened, I shut my eyes to make them go away.

When I next wake, day's come and Bunny is calling me from the next room. 'Mamma. Mamma.'

I get up wearily and stumble into the kitchen to make him his bottle.

I wait till mid-morning before I telephone Bryn.

Sonia answers so I don't say anything but she knows it's me. 'Maddie? Is that you? Madeleine?'

Her voice hasn't changed. That's what's so bad. The way she says my name. Something inside me whispers, insidious, she still loves you, you're still her dead friend's daughter but Bryn, Bryn…and I drop the phone because her love diminishes me, makes me a little girl still and she ought to know, she ought to know better than anyone that I'm not.

Except…except…Bryn has gone back to her. Tom. Oliver. Sonia. They are a family again. It's like it didn't mean anything, Bryn and me. His hands on my breasts, his eyes, the hunger in his face and me laughing, 'I am La Belle Dame sans Merci, aren't I?' and afterwards, afterwards…

I put my hands across my face and start to sob. Sonia's right. I am a little girl and it's easy for her to go on loving me because she's got him and I haven't.

*

Bryn rings me in the afternoon. I know it's him, no one else ever rings me, so I scoop Bunny up from the floor where he's playing with his truck and dump him in his cot. He whimpers a bit but I frown at him and he settles down immediately, his thumb in his mouth, his other hand groping for his cuddly.

I run back into the kitchen and snatch up the handset. 'Bryn. Oh, Bryn.'

'I told you not to ring here, Madeleine.'

'Bunny,' I whisper. 'It's Bunny. He…'

'What's wrong with Bunny? He's not ill, is he?'

'No, but…' I begin again. 'He's your son. He needs to see you.'

'Look, I've told you. When he's older, we'll work something out. At the moment that's impossible. Sonia…'

In front of me, Bunny's truck, his scattered blocks. Their colours blur and run together and I shake my head and turn quickly away.

'I can't look after Bunny by myself.'

'Don't start that again. I'm paying you a very generous allowance for him, far more than you are entitled to. Besides, you have options. We've been through them.'

'They're stupid. Going back to university. Getting a job. How will that change anything? Bunny'll still be here at the end of it and you'll be off with Sonia and the boys, free of me but I, I won't ever…'

'Madeleine…'

'Anyway, I'm not staying here. I hate it here. I want to go to the beach shack.'

'I don't think that's a good idea.'

'Why not? You're not going there, are you?' I stop, my mind a confusion of images, shared holidays before my mother died, Dad fishing from the rocks with my brother Peter, Sonia and Mum laughing, the tide coming in laced with foam, Oliver with a bucket of little blue spider crabs. 'Please,' I whisper. 'Just for a few weeks, just until I work out what I'm going to do.'

'Well, maybe, but I…I can't drive you down. You must understand that. Perhaps…'

My voice changes. 'You're afraid, aren't you? You're afraid to be alone with me because you know if you are…'

'Don't be ridiculous.'

There's an odd little silence. Outside, a dog barking. Birds. A car door slamming.

'Maybe Julian…'

'My father won't speak to me.' I turn towards the window. Across the little square lawn, shadows. Evening coming on fast, too fast. 'Peter will take me, though. He's got his licence now and Dad'll lend him the car just so long as he doesn't know it's for me'.

'All right then.' I've worn him down. His voice is suddenly old, defeated

Triumph. I ought to feel triumphant but…but…

'You send Peter round and I'll give him the keys.'

I put the phone back and go into the bedroom to check on Bunny. Even asleep with his thumb in his mouth and his fingers splayed out across his cheek, he looks like Bryn and I start to shudder again like I did when I woke in the night.

*

As soon as it's light enough, I run down to the beach. The sea's flat calm, silver where it meets the sky but darker close to the shore where the rocks are. Sandals dangling from my hand, I make my way carefully to the water's edge. Colour's beginning. Pink shells. A line of white foam. A child's red ribbon. I bend down to pick up a piece of sea glass coloured like smoke.

At the other end of the cove, where the cliffs jut into the sea, men with a boat. Gulls. A cormorant on a rock holding out wings like bits of broken umbrella. Dawn is over. It's morning. Sighing, I turn and go back up through the sand dunes to the shack.

Bunny's asleep. He's been crying, though; his lashes are wet against the curve of his cheek.

'I'm sorry,' I whisper. 'I never…' My throat goes tight so I have to start again. 'It wasn't meant to be like this, you and me by ourselves. Bryn said… Bryn promised…'

Bunny whimpers in his sleep and turns his head away. For just a moment I want to grab him up and hold him my baby, oh! my baby, but there are other things inside me too and I hear myself cry out, 'I would never have let you be born if I'd known he was going to leave me.'

I stumble outside again, my hand over my mouth. Now I've said it, I can't take it back.

*

I load Bunny into his stroller and push him up the hill and across to the little cluster of shops. I buy him a yellow floppy hat and look around for a bucket and spade. 'You'll need them for the beach,' I tell him. 'You can dig, dig in the sand and...'

He's not listening. He's got his cuddly up against his cheek and he's crooning to it like he does when he's in his cot.

'What about a ball? You like balls, don't you?'

He still doesn't say anything so I get the things and, tight-mouthed, cram them into my backpack.

I turn the stroller round and set off for home. Below us, the sunlit sea, the dark, jumbled rocks, the pink and yellow shacks. To the left of the cove where the cliffs are friendlier, the little reed-fringed lagoon.

'It's good here,' I say desperately. 'You'll like it, Bunny. I know you will.'

His new hat hides his face so it's easier to talk to him. I take a deep breath and quicken my pace.

Later, after his sleep, I pack a picnic tea and take Bunny down to the beach. Once we're past the sandhills, he lets go of my hand and stands very still, staring. Sea and sky. The pale wet sand. A spume of spindrift flung up above the rocks.

He turns, tilting his head back to look at me. 'Beach? Bunny go beach?'

Something happens inside me. An aching. I catch him up and hold him so close I can feel the separate beating of our hearts. 'I told you it was good here,' I whisper. 'I told you...'

I set him down on a patch of sand and tip his toys out of my backpack. His dump truck. The boat Peter got him for his birthday. His new bucket and spade.

'See,' I say. 'You dig like this. Sand. You put it in your bucket.'

He takes no notice, though. Instead, he picks up his own fistful of sand and watches it slide through his fingers. The closed look's on his face; he's never had it so strong before but Bryn did, all the time in those last few weeks when he was remembering Sonia and wishing he was holding her and not me.

I jump up and go over to the rocks. I sit down with my back to him, my chin resting on my humped knees. 'Medea,' I say so loud I startle myself. 'Was it like this for you too, after Jason left, something broken so that when you looked at your children you didn't see them, only him?' My voice drops to a whisper. 'I was so glad when Bunny was born. I...I cried. It seemed such a wondrous thing to have a son, to be joined to someone else. I thought...I thought...'

Suddenly I lean forward and jab my fingers into the damp sand. 'Bryn didn't feel the same, did he? Any more than Jason. Everything you did, even...even killing your own brother, it wasn't enough for Jason and, and all the things I did...my father...my father won't ever forgive me... Bryn, Bryn was his friend and he feels...he feels...'

I stop and it's a while before I can go on. 'Bunny,' I whisper. 'It's worse because of Bunny. Bryn doesn't want him any more than he wants me.'

I get up and go down to the water's edge. Medea goes with me. She doesn't say anything but I know she's there watching the little waves turn themselves over and over till they disappear in a swirl of foam.

*

Mornings are best. The brightening sky. The sun on the water. I settle Bunny with his toys and go down over the rocks. I find things for him. Shells. Coloured stones. Bleached coral. Once, a shark's egg with petals like leather. When I give them to him, Bunny examines each one, turning it over in his hands and crooning to it as if it's alive. Then, solemn-eyed, he puts them carefully into his bucket for me to take back to the shack.

Things are different once we're there, though. Something's gone out of the day. A brightness. Bunny sleeps most of the afternoon and I, suddenly restless, go from room to room picking up things and putting them down again. A jug of dried grasses. A painted tea caddy. A broken china horse. Discarded, I think, wincing; things like us that no one wants...

I find a pile of old books in the back of the kitchen cupboard. *Heidi.*
The Old Curiosity Shop. Lorna Doone. What Maisie Knew. Northanger Abbey.
That one's got my mother's name in it. Lydia Kennedy. St Margaret's
Girls' Grammar School 1973. The writing's thin, spiked, oddly familiar,
and I trace over it trying to connect myself to her, my mother who died
when I was thirteen. 'Mum,' I say aloud. 'Mum…'

Behind me then Medea, the sudden hiss of her indrawn breath. 'What
are you talking to her for? She won't understand. How can she? Your
father loved her. Even when she was dying and no use to him, he kept
on loving her.'

I slam the book shut and whirl around to face her but I'm too late.
The kitchen's quite empty, the bare floor in front of me striped only with
the thin shadows from the bamboo blind across the window.

*

Dawn at last. In the trees behind the shack, the little wild birds. I squeeze
my eyes shut. I know what I have to do but I don't want to think about it.

I pull on my shorts and T-shirt and go into Bunny's room. Asleep, he
looks smaller, his arms flung up above his head like when he was a baby, his
lashes dark against the curve of his cheeks, his mouth half-open, uncertain.

My voice comes out harsher than I intend. 'Come on, Bunny. It's time
to get up.'

He blinks himself awake and sits up to stare at me. 'Beach? San'?'

I don't answer him. I can't. Instead I sort out his clothes and, once
he's dressed, I take him into the kitchen for breakfast. I stand by the
window drinking coffee while he busies himself with his toast.

Outside, all the birds are quiet and the pink is going from the sky…

'Hurry up. It's getting late.'

The beach is deserted. Over by the cliffs, gulls, but the fishermen
have already left. I put Bunny down, relieved. Colour's come into the sky,
there's a tenderness to it, and the sea, stretched out between the cliffs,
is like a piece of silk, shot silk that I saw once in a retro shop window,
grey but other colours too, blue and violet, shadows and little spreading
glitters of light. I take a deep breath. It isn't real. None of it's real. Bryn.
His hands. His mouth. His eyes…

I lift my chin. 'Soon,' I whisper. 'Soon it won't matter. It'll be like it never happened…'

Bunny pulls at my hand. 'Mamma. San'. Bunny play san'.'

'No.' I pick him up again. 'Not today,' and, kicking off my sandals, I go down to the water's edge.

The tide's going out. I watch it a moment and then I make myself go forward. So many things. It's like I'm seeing them for the first time. The little translucent waves. Limpets on a ridge of rock. A darting silver fish. Over against the cliffs, a surge of white spray.

'Stars,' I whisper. 'Falling stars.'

Further out, the sea changes. It's darker now, angry; it swirls around us and I have to hoist Bunny higher in my arms and tread water to keep us afloat. Bunny's frightened. He's whimpering, his breath coming in little painful gasps, my baby, oh! my baby, but I have to…I have to… Medea… and I turn my head away and let him go. He reaches out for me. For one moment I feel his little clutching hands but then it's all right, the sea's taken him and I'm myself again, Madeleine Barton. I can go on where I left off. The university. The shifting shadows under the ash trees. The lawns sloping down to the river. The library…I am eighteen again and it never happened, none of it happened and Bryn, Bryn is married to Sonia, my mother's friend, and we never…we never …

The water's shallower now, friendly. I laugh with relief and when I look up I see her, the lady Medea, down by the rocks. She's bending forward and singing to herself. When I call out to her, she lifts her head and smiles. Her eyes, elongated with kohl, meet mine. They're fierce and dark and quite, quite mad and I start to shudder so hard I have to stop and wrap my arms around myself to keep myself from falling.

Birds

She can't sleep. She turns her head, whimpering, on the pillow. Pictures of her life come back so she's a little girl again squatting in the dirt making pictures out of pine fronds and marigold flowers.

She's on her way home from school, whispering stories to herself, but the big boys have seen her. They laugh and point and call out names and one, the tallest, bends down and sends a skittering of gravel after her. She's scared, she wants to run, she feels it quivering in her legs…run, run…but she's a big girl now, seven and a half and that's too old, far too old, and she goes on with her story till she's crossed the railway line and the boys have disappeared, laughing, down a side street.

She's ten, eleven. Her mother's plaiting her hair, the ends turned up and bound with coloured cotton, and she holds her head very still and watches the dust motes dancing in a sudden shaft of sunlight.

High school. Sonia Davis with her narrow, delicately boned face and eloquent hands, 'Let's be friends,' and she, wide-eyed, nodding and afterwards writing in her diary, 'It's like the sun set in a welter of green and violet. So unexpected.'

Saturday afternoons at the public library together. Stippled sunlight on the river. Black swans with a family of half-grown cygnets. Wind in the reeds. A child with a red balloon.

Exams. Sonia, impatient, 'Of course you'll pass,' and, afterwards, waiting in the darkness before dawn for the heart-stopping thud of the newspaper. Opening the front door. The pinkening sky. The cold grass. Inside again…her hands shaking….numbers so many numbers…why, oh why, don't they use words…words are real…friendly…algebra's all right but maths is nearly her downfall.

Suddenly university…the train…there's a man on the train…his face…she watches him covertly from under her eyelashes…she wants his face to mean something but of course it's only another one of her stories.

But…she's back in the present again…her room…the familiar, friendly shadows in the corners. Anton wasn't a story. Anton was real… only now…

'Oh,' she whispers, clenching her hands. 'Oh, if only none of it were real, twenty years, and I was on the train going into university and all my life ahead of me, unlived.'

Her wedding day. Early morning. She slips outside through the silent, sleeping house to a garden hazed with light. A dew-wet leaf. The blue and white agapanthus along the driveway. A drooping, full-blown rose. She touches it with suddenly tender fingers. 'I am not myself,' she thinks. 'And after today I won't ever be myself again. I'll be…I'll be his wife.'

She feels herself shudder…or is it the rose…its petals scattering even as she draws back her hand. But…but… 'Delight,' she says fiercely. 'I am shuddering in delight.' She loves him and 'love obliterates' and her head goes up and she whispers, 'Love means I'm not myself. I'm him and he… he …'

Afterwards, bemused, in her wedding dress, chiffon edged with lace, her hair loose down her back. Her mother hands her her bouquet, a few frangipani tied with white ribbon, and covers her face with her wedding veil.

She hears herself cry out in her bed and her hands go up to her mouth to block it out…the pain…the pain of remembering when…when…

The vows. His voice so sure. She couldn't have been mistaken. He meant it then. With this ring, I thee wed. With my body, I thee worship. But…but…afterwards…he was different afterwards… She wasn't special any more.

'And…and if he marries her, will it be the same or will he be able to go on loving her when she's his wife because if he does…if he does it means it's my fault not his…'

She bites at her lip till her mouth is full of the taste of blood. 'I have to find a way to get back to myself… All these years, all I've been is his wife, their mother.' She stops then. The children. She whispers their names like an incantation. Caitlin. Beau. Gretta. Alicia-Rose. Nathan. Danny. Even that's changed, though. The older ones don't need her; they're almost grown up and even the little boys…soon…soon…

In a corner of her room, Danny in his cot. The day after Anton left, Alicia-Rose had helped her shift it there. 'I should have a room of my own,' she'd said, hard-mouthed. 'Caitlin and Gretta don't have to share with anyone.'

'But…'

'Dad's gone. You can have him in here now. He's your baby, not mine.'

She doesn't know this new Alicia-Rose. She doesn't know any of them. Anton's going has changed them all.

Once…children…it's like they were all children together and now they've grown up and they've become suddenly aware she hasn't… They've gone beyond her…nineteen, seventeen, fifteen, fourteen, and she's a child still with Nathan and Danny but soon enough they'll grow beyond her too and she'll… She shudders. She's frightened now…the years ahead, oh the bleak years ahead, and she puts her hands across her face, sobbing.

'I used to be…' but it's lost to her. She no longer knows how to define herself. If she is not Anton's wife, the children's mother, she is no one at all.

Inside the window frame, the beginning of light. She reaches a hand out to touch the smooth, plastered wall for reassurance. Dawn. Dawn at last.

She gets up quickly, pulls on her dress, sandals, combs her fingers through her hair. She's at the door by the cot… Danny asleep on his stomach clutching his blanket…tenderness…oh! Whatever else she has lost, still this tenderness for her baby. Her mother, tight-lipped, 'Pity you ever had those last two. Such a big gap between them and Alicia-Rose and now look at you, left with them still on your hands.' She pushes her fist back into her mouth. 'No, no. she's wrong. I need them. Oh God, I need them.'

She goes through into the kitchen, down the passage and she's outside. Behind the house, the dark-rimmed hills, but over to the east a spill of pink and gold light. She sits down at the picnic table and tilts her head back to watch the brightening sky. The wonder of it fills her and she's suddenly calm. 'I'll be all right. I'll find a way to get back to myself. He's gone but it wasn't any good. In the end it wasn't any good for either of us.'

On the lawn under the apple tree, a flock of starlings. She watches them, frowning. Insects, she thinks; there must be insects in the grass. The light flows over them like water, they're black, they're brown, they're limned with gold. Suddenly, all at once, they take fright and are gone.

'But...but...' Always at school – poetry, Icarus flying too close to the sun, Jonathon Livingstone Seagull – birds were for freedom... independence. 'But they're not free. How can they be when they take fright so suddenly and there's nothing there? They were safe... the grass...the tree...but they thought...' She shakes her head. 'They're not free at all, only brave. Courage,' she thinks. 'I thought it was Beauty and Truth like in Keats' poem, another bit, somewhere there was another bit, the swallows gathering, the sky – I can't remember – but...but it's courage I need and it can't be so hard. The birds...so brave the birds, and so beautiful.'

Her head jerks up and her mouth is suddenly resolute. 'I'll write it down about the birds, the starlings. I used to like writing things, I don't even know why I stopped, but I'll start again and it'll be something, something for me.'

She sits very still. The light so tender on the new-leafed apple tree and after a while, in little tentative groups, the birds start to come back.

Red Blanket

The girl Marion's dreaming about has just had a baby. She's in a room with a lot of other young mothers; it's impossible to tell how many because the edges of the dream run into one another like the colours in a child's painting. She's got the baby wrapped in a bright red blanket and she sits on her bed, rocking it and humming to herself.

One of the other women, the one in the opposite cubicle, lifts her baby out of its little plastic cot. It looks too big to be newborn, too bright-eyed. The girl goes suddenly still. Oh! Tufts of dark hair. Little round arms and legs. One small, out-thrust starfish hand. The girl catches her breath and watches its mother open the fastenings of her nightdress and put it to her breast.

Then the midwife's there, bending over them. 'Yes,' she says, nodding approval. 'That's the way.' She moves to another mother and then another but when she gets to the girl with the red blanket, she walks past her, head held high, as if she hasn't seen her. The girl doesn't care; she shrugs and goes on with her rocking.

After a while, the other mother, having finished attending to her child and returned it to its cot, comes over to her. 'Did you have a little boy or a little girl?' she asks, smiling, friendly. 'We've all been wondering ever since you came in last night.'

The girl looks up, startled, and her eyes go very wide. 'I...I don't know. I don't think they said.' Then, suddenly resolute, she squares her shoulders. 'It's a boy. I'm sure it's a boy because that's what I wanted.' She smiles, and it's a child's smile, pleading. 'Everyone always wants a boy first, don't they?'

The other mother frowns and takes a step or two backward. Then she can't help herself. 'Why have you got him wrapped like that?' she demands, pursing up her mouth. 'You can't even see his face.'

The girl clutches her bundle tighter. 'He's just been born. They said…
they said I mustn't let him get cold or…'

'But it's so warm in here. Our babies…' She turns, indicating, and it's
true, the other babies are gurgling and kicking in their cribs, bare-limbed,
dressed only in nappies and little hand-smocked shirts.

The girl's face goes stubborn. 'He's my baby. He likes it like this.'

'Aren't you going to feed him, then? It's already past ten o'clock.'

'All right. I will. Go away and I will.' She puts the baby on the bed
next to her and starts to fumble with the buttons on her nightdress. Even
open, though, her nightdress is too restricting and in the end she slips it
down carefully over her shoulders so both her breasts are exposed. They
are small and immature, a young girl's breasts, and the other mother, still
watching, makes a little moue of disdain. The girl doesn't notice. She's
leaning forward, cupping one breast in her hands, her face absorbed and
very still.

The light that has wavered uncertainly around the room, touching
first one face and then another, concentrates itself at last on the girl, her
delicate profile, her fall of pale hair, the sweet innocence of her breasts
and narrow shoulders.

She turns and picks the bundle up from the bed and the blanket falls
away. It isn't a baby at all. It's a large rag doll, badly made; the other
mother can see its clumsily stitched mouth and its staring, button eyes.

Marion, dreaming on her bed, starts to whimper. She tries to make the
dream change, one of her stories that she can give any ending she likes,
but this is a dream and she can't; she tries but she can't make the doll turn
into a real baby, pink and plump-limbed, it keeps on being a doll, ugly and
misshapen, and, in her distress, she moans aloud.

The girl…the girl who might or might not be her… Marion shudders
and goes on watching as the girl holds the doll to her breast, frowning
when she sees it doesn't open its mouth. 'Never mind,' she says at last.
'You don't have to if you don't want to. It doesn't matter.'

'Don't be ridiculous,' says the other mother, affronted. 'It's a doll.
Can't you see it's a doll? You shouldn't be here with us, not when all
you've got is that stupid, stuffed doll.'

The girl leaps to her feet. Her eyes, dilated, are a deer's eyes, Bambi in
the forest, hunted, but she's proud too, she's got a brittle childish dignity.

'You are hateful,' she shouts. 'All of you. What is it to you what I have? You've got your babies.' Her voice quivers and almost breaks. 'Why can't you…why can't you…' She doesn't finish. She throws the doll onto the bed behind her and runs from the room, her hands across her face, sobbing.

Marion stirs, mutters something, flings out an arm and she's awake, sitting up, bemused. The morning light, through the gauze curtains, lies across the bed in swaths, and she reaches out an uncertain hand as if to catch it and hold it safe. Then, all in one movement, she gets up and shrugs herself into her dressing gown. She goes over to stand by the window. Sharp shadows of trees, sparrows on the lawn, a falling leaf. She puts her arms across her stomach and feels, for the first time, her baby stir inside her. Her eyes, still watching the birds outside, go wide with wonder.

It's spring when her baby is born. They let her hold him for a little while before, with sad faces, they take him quietly away.

Marion cries out just once and then, her fist in her mouth, she flings herself back on her bed. 'I hoped…' she whispers and then she stops suddenly. She's remembered the girl with the red blanket. It's like she's there too, in the doorway, watching. In the white, brightly lit room, she seems smaller, insubstantial, her delicately boned face raddled with tears.

'Oh. Oh.' Marion turns herself to the wall and begins to weep for them both.

White Noise

Morning. Maja wakes up and she knows. She's pregnant. Outside, a blackbird singing and the light falling in stripes across her bed. She puts her hand up through the slatted blind to touch the window-pane. The glass so cold. It's like she's never touched it before. The uneven plaster of the wall. The white-painted windowsill. Her spider plant. Her little pottery lamp. Everything the same and everything different.

It started when she first met Callum. April then; the leaves falling, red and orange and burgundy. She'd reached up to catch one and it quivered in her hands like something alive and, smiling to herself, she went down to the river. It was her place. School. Caroline's party that she'd run away from the night before. Home. Her father frowning. The empty space where her mother ought to be but wasn't because she'd died before Maja could remember. None of it mattered here. Not by the river. Only the light on the water. The birds. A shudder of wind in the reeds.

She'd thrown her leaf into the water and watched the current take it downstream. By the bridge there was a man she'd never seen before. He was hunched over a sketch pad drawing, his hair over his face and she had started to walk toward him, she couldn't help herself. When she got close enough to see him properly, the curve of his cheek, his taut mouth, he looked up and smiled and just like that, everything changed. Her whole world. Herself. Sky and sun and the sweet, sweet grass, the river, the willow fronds trailing in the water... Everything.

And now... She lets her hands rest for a moment on her stomach. 'Oh,' she whispers. 'Oh.' The baby's suddenly there in her mind. She sees him in a wicker basket she's lined with white lace, just the top of his head in a swaddle of blankets and one out-thrust, star-shaped hand. He's propped up in a corner of the sofa. He's bigger now. His hair is silky-soft, a tangle of curls, his eyes are blue like Callum's, a blue so dark it looks black and when he sees her, he smiles and holds out his arms. He's staggering after them at the beach and when Callum bends to scoop him up, she can see behind them, his little wet footprints in the sand…

Maja sits up and pushes the hair out of her eyes. 'Oh,' she whispers again. 'Oh.' She feels her heart turn over. He's already real.

She gets up quickly and pulls on her school skirt and a clean shirt. Then she goes into the bathroom to splash water on her face. She gropes for a towel and her face looks back at her, frowning, from the mirror. A child's face. Eager. Expectant. Dark eyes and a tangle of gypsy curls. She doesn't want to look like that. Not any more. She wants…

She sighs. Callum thinks she's a child. She's seen it too often in his face, an amused tenderness. Despite everything, passion, his hands touching her, his lips on her throat, her breasts, despite… Her cheeks burn at the images her mind gives her, despite all that… 'He thinks I'm still a little girl,' she tells her reflection. 'That's why I wanted a baby. To prove to him.' Her head jerks up suddenly. 'To prove to them all.'

Because they're wrong. Her father. Her older sister Stephanie. Her school friends. Callum. Even the mirror. Maja Wilson. None of them know her. How can they? She's not herself any more. Not the self she was because…She clutches hold of the towel-rail to steady herself. Suddenly she's laughing and she turns and runs into the kitchen where her father's already cooking breakfast.

*

The apple tree in the front garden's in bloom. She turns back at the gate to look at it. It's a bride, she thinks, smiling, her father's old tree, gnarled, twisted, but now in spring, it's young again.

'Tonight,' she whispers. 'Tonight I'll tell Callum.' She stops again. 'Did you hear that?' she tells the baby. 'Tonight I'm going to tell your father about you.'

She tilts back her head. Above her, the sky is wide and blue, endless, she thinks and she remembers suddenly Callum setting up his easel in the front room of the derelict cottage he's taken over. 'See, Maja. See how the sky's full of light now it's stopped raining.' She laughs aloud and shoulders her backpack. She'll be late for school if she doesn't hurry. Laughing, she

66

starts to run. She's like the apple tree. Her time has come and nothing can hold it back.

*

She's lived with it all day but when she gets there, she doesn't know how to begin. Callum in the cottage doorway, backlit, and she's suddenly shy but then she's in his arms, he's kissing her and she can feel his heart beating. My heart, she thinks fiercely because they did it last year in English, 'my true love hath my heart and I have his'. She didn't know what it meant then but she does now.

She makes herself pull away. 'Callum…' She's not sure he's heard. He's already halfway across the room. 'Come and see my painting. It's turned out even better than I expected. I'm bound to win the Country Arts Prize now, and then, in the summer, I'll be able to go down the coast…' Her heart. His heart. It's beating so loud she has to raise her voice to hear herself above it. 'I've got something to tell you. Something important.'

'Yeah? What's up?'

'I…' Then, all in a rush, 'I'm pregnant.'

'What?'

'I'm…I'm going to have a baby.'

Two steps and he's there, too close, and his eyes, oh God, his eyes…

'What do you mean, a baby?'

'Don't…oh, Callum, don't look like that.'

'I told you. I told you from the beginning. No ties. No commitments. You agreed. You said you understood. You said you wanted it like that too.'

All at once his voice breaks, is a boy's voice betrayed and she hears it and puts her hand out to him but it's only for a moment, almost immediately he's a man again, a man she doesn't know and she flinches from him.

'You said you'd take care of everything, it would be your responsibility, you'd go to a doctor, get a prescription…'

'I did, Callum. I…'

'Then how did this happen? Tell me that, Maja. How did this happen?' He's got hold of her now, his hands rough on her shoulders, wrenching her round to face him. 'Don't lie to me, Maja. Tell me how you can be pregnant if you did what I said.'

Suddenly it's easy. The words spill out of her. They have a cadence to them like the poetry she loves. 'I haven't told you properly, not everything. Because a baby…don't you see, a baby's part of it, part of us loving each other. It's…it's the culmination. When you love someone, like, like we do, well, a baby's the proof. It's like one of your paintings. It shows…it shows what love means.'

His mouth tightens and she thinks he's going to answer but instead he pushes her away and goes over to the window.

'I did go to the doctor,' she whispers at last. 'I got the prescription like you said but after a while I stopped taking it. I thought…' She runs to him then and puts a hand on his arm. 'You have to listen to me. It'll be all right. I know it will. I'll look after it, the baby. It won't get in the way. I understand about your work, really I do, but we won't need much, the baby and me, just as long as we're together, all of us, Callum, a family.'

He doesn't move. 'No,' he says. 'No, I told you. I've been through all that. Marriage. A mortgage. Kids. Shit, Maja, how many times do I have to tell you? It didn't work with her and it won't work with you.'

'You don't know that. I'm not her. You said that once…you said…'

'I want to paint. I have to. I'm not giving it up. Not for you. Not for anyone.'

'I don't want you to. I just told you.' Her hands go out to him again before she can stop them. 'You…you said you loved me…when we… afterwards, you always say you love me.'

He laughs then, turning, his face dark and cruel…a wolf. Oh God, God, a wolf leaping… 'Of course I did. Why not? You were all over me. Wide-eyed. A kid. I said what you wanted me to.'

'Then…then…'

'Leave it, Maja. We've got to decide now what you're going to do.'

She turns her head away. She can't hear him. Something else, though. She struggles to make sense of it…inside her head, noise, white noise. 'Ice,' she whispers. 'Ice breaking up,' and she wonders how she knows when it's not something she's ever heard. The sea, so dark and treacherous, the sea between the ice-packs…you wouldn't think…and the ice so hard and white and lonely. A sudden splinter of quivering light, blue and violet, rose-pink, oh, oh, and then it's gone again and there's only the noise…the dreadful, dreadful noise and the broken, jagged ice.

Shuddering, she puts her hands over her ears. She wants it to stop, she has to make it stop because…

'I have to go home,' and, running, she reaches the door and wrenches it open.

'Maja, Maja, wait a minute.'

Outside it's quite dark. She hesitates, disconcerted. Just a little while ago, she was running along the river path and behind the hills the light was like liquid gold. She'd stopped to watch it, the heavy clouds and the light…the light…

'Maja…'

She's reached the broken front fence and she grasps hold of a paling, panting. 'Running,' she thinks, frowning. 'I've been running. The river, I was running by the river. I threw my leaf into the water and then I looked up and saw… No, no that was April because the leaves… It's October now. Spring. The bulrushes are in flower, they're like brown velvet. Callum and I picked some so he could paint them.' She shakes her head…the noise…the noise…it's hard to think because of the noise. Even now, when she can't see the breaking ice floes, she can still hear them and the crying…the gulls…the crying gulls…

'I have to go home.'

Suddenly it's all right. Home. Her father's home and their old dog Mikki, her room, her books on her desk, her spider plant, her little pottery lamp. Stephanie bought it for her years ago because, after their mother died, she used to wake, crying in the dark. Stephanie'd come in and light the lamp and they'd watch it together, the little flickering flame so brave…

She lifts her head. The darkness beats around her like it's got wings but ahead, where the main road is, she can see the street-lights. She lets go of the fence and stumbles toward them with a little incoherent cry.

'Bless me, Father...'

When we reach the cathedral steps, Emma pulls her hand out of mine and says, 'It's still early. Can't we...can't we go by the fountain and wait a while.'

I frown. 'I don't think...'

But she's insistent. 'Please,' she says and then she turns quickly and starts back down the street.

She bends her head so her hair falls over her face. She has long hair, very fine, and in the sun it gleams more gold than brown. Looking at it, I feel the familiar constricting of my heart and I hurry after her.

We don't say anything when we reach the fountain. Emma stands with her back to me, watching the water. She's crying. I'm not sure what to do. It's ridiculous. She's not a child. I turn abruptly and go to examine the memorial plaque at the entrance to the park.

After a while, I notice that Emma has sat down on the stone coping round the fountain. She's trailing her hand in the water. I go back to her.

She doesn't look up but she knows I'm there because she says, 'I don't think... Rick, I can't do this.' Her voice is steady enough but then her eyes, desperate, seek mine. 'Please, Rick,' she says again. 'Please, I can't.'

I'm angry. I try to hide it but she knows because I see her flinch. She takes her hand out of the water and starts pleating the folds of her dress.

'You promised, Emma,' I say. I take a deep breath. 'And it's not only me. You know that. It's my family. We...' I shake my head and sit down next to her but I won't let myself touch her. 'I thought you understood. You said you did. My family will never accept me marrying out of my faith. You said it was all right. You said you wanted us to believe the same things. And our children. You wanted...' I pause a moment and then I add, 'You gave your word.'

'I know.' She bites her lip. 'And I will. I will.' She's stopped crying but her face is still red and blotched. She's ugly when she cries.

I say coldly, 'Then why are you making such a fuss?'

'I...' She shakes her hair out of her eyes. 'It isn't easy. I mean, most things I don't mind telling...you know, like lying to my mother and being mean to Rachel when she annoys me and even things like not always believing in God and when we miss Mass on Sundays because we've both got assignments due. I'm sure I can tell the priest things like that. It's us. I don't know how I can tell the priest about us...put into words that you and I have...that we've actually... I don't know how I can say that. And I have to. Father Martin said you have to confess everything especially when it's a mortal sin and...I don't mind telling God. I mean, He knows already, doesn't He? but I don't know how I can tell anyone else.'

'It's the same thing, though. Father Martin must have told you that. The priest represents God. Anyway, I don't see why you're so upset. The priest won't know you. That's why Father Martin said to come here – so we'd be anonymous.'

Emma looks down at her hands. 'I can't,' she whispers. 'I just can't.'

I get up. 'I should think you'd mind more, sitting here crying where everyone can see you. I'm telling you, it's no big deal. Thousands of people do it. Even kids. You know that. My little sister, Francie, she never carries on like this.' I can't help it. There's an edge to my voice. I force myself to continue more gently. 'Look, you know what to do. You go in. You can't see the priest so it's like he isn't there. You can tell yourself that anyway. You say, "Bless me, Father, for I have sinned..." You tell him you're a convert and this is your first confession.' I shrug and try to smile at her. 'I have to do it too. You've forgotten that, haven't you? I have to as well. Now, come on, we've wasted enough time.'

She sighs but she gets up and follows me.

I wait for her at the cathedral steps. She doesn't say anything even when I take her hand.

'It'll be all right,' I say, more to reassure myself than her.

She gives me a small smile. It's like most of her smiles. It stops before it reaches her eyes. I know why. Bad things have happened to her and I'm sorry but it's different now. She's got me. She doesn't have to let things get to her so much.

There's a lot of people ahead of us. I clench my jaw. I hate waiting around.

I turn to Emma. 'When it's our turn,' I whisper, 'you go first.'

She lifts her head. Her eyes are big and dark and sort of unfocused. She nods. Then she goes back to her praying.

When she comes out, she doesn't look at me. She's enclosed in silence. You can almost see it like an aura. But by the time I've finished and join her to say my penance, she's herself again.

'I'm going to light a candle,' she says suddenly and she gets up and goes to the altar.

I finish my last Hail Mary and follow her. She's kneeling down. Her eyes, watching the flickering flames, are bright as a child's at Christmas.

She chooses a candle and lights it. 'Look, Rick,' she whispers. 'It's praying for us.'

We go out into the sunshine.

Emma tilts her head back and stares into the sky. 'Oh, Rick,' she says. 'Look what sort of day we've got.' She starts to spin round, her arms outstretched. 'Oh, Rick, it was worth it just to feel like this.'

I don't know what to say.

She grabs both my hands and tries to pull me round with her. 'Absolution,' she says. 'You never said it would feel like this.'

'Well, I guess…' I begin but she isn't listening.

'He wanted me to go and see him,' she says, clutching at my arm to steady herself. 'He said if I ever wanted to discuss anything, I could make an appointment. I think it's because I told him I don't believe what we're doing is wrong. I told him we love one another and we're getting married next year when you've got your degree so I don't see why…' She pauses for a moment. 'Did you tell him that too?' She giggles. 'I wonder if he realised who you were. You know, that you were the one I was talking about.'

'You didn't say my name, did you? Father Martin told you, you don't say names…'

'Of course not. Though it wouldn't matter. He's not allowed to let himself identify us, is he? I mean, not even if we're his own parishioners.'

'All the same, you don't give names. And you didn't have to go into all that detail. All you had to say was…'

'I had to say how I felt.'

'Yes, but…'

Emma's frowning now. She's gone suddenly serious. 'What did you say, Rick? Exactly? What did you tell him?'

I feel uncomfortable. But I have to answer. She has that effect on me. I'm always telling her things I've never told anyone else. 'I just said, sometimes my girlfriend and I have gone a bit too far.'

Her eyes are wide and very blue. They shame me. She says slowly. 'But that's not…'

I kiss her quickly to distract her. To distract both of us. Then I grab her hand and we go to the library where we usually spend Saturdays studying so we can have the rest of the weekend free.

Play In Three Acts

Amy is almost asleep when she hears Jason come home. She keeps her eyes closed and turns her head restlessly on the pillow but it isn't any use. She has to get up and confront him.

He's in the kitchen, his back to her, examining the contents of the open refrigerator. She hears her voice say, as if from a great distance, 'Jason, you're back. I've been waiting for you.'

He turns then. He's got a can of beer in his hand and, while she watches, he opens it and takes a gulp, his eyes all the time appraising her. 'Well,' he says, smiling slowly. 'Well.'

Amy's mouth tightens. 'Come into the lounge,' she says. 'I've got something to tell you. It's important.'

Shrugging, Jason follows and flings himself into the nearest chair. Amy takes a deep breath. She doesn't look at him, though. She daren't. Instead she watches her hands in her lap. They're so small, her hands. Small and defenceless.

Amy's lips quiver and she lifts her head. 'I went to see Mum today,' she says. 'I had to. I had to tell her.'

'So?'

'She said, she said I ought to…it'd be better if I didn't have it. She said it isn't a baby yet, not really and if I went to the clinic, they could… It wouldn't take long, I wouldn't even have to stay in overnight and then, then…' Her eyes, desperate, search Jason's face but he makes no response and her voice drops to a whisper. 'It's the only way, she said, 'with Timmy still so young, it's the only way I'll be able to manage and…'

Jason's lip curls. 'Your mother! Who cares what your mother thinks? Whingeing old cow!'

Amy shakes her head. All at once her voice is very steady. 'She knows, though. She knows what it'll be like. She had me and Krystal close together. Thirteen months. She said it was bad. She couldn't look after us properly. Dad wasn't any help. He'd just had his accident so he was off work and there wasn't enough money and one of us was always crying. I don't want that for Timmy. I want him to have…'

'Oh, shut up about your mother. It'll be different for us. And there's social security. They'll look after us. Fact, it'll be easier. More kids we have, the more money they'll give us.'

'But…'

'And I'll get a job. Robbo told me there's something going at the mill. He's gonna put in a good word for me.'

Amy's head jerks up but before she can say anything, Jason begins to shout, 'You couldn't expect me to stay on at the vineyard. Six o'clock every morning no matter the weather and that bloody foreman always picking on me.'

'It's not the money,' Amy whispers, her eyes on her hands. 'It's… it's me. I can't cope with two. I know I can't. It's bad enough with one. You're out all the time with your mates. You, you don't know what it's like. I feel…I feel like I'm being swallowed up, like…' She lifts her head. 'Sometimes I feel like I'm, like I'm…'

'Oh, for crying out loud.' Jason leaps to his feet. 'Do what you want. I'm going to bed.'

Amy doesn't answer. She watches her hands pluck at the folds of her nightdress. At last she looks up. Her eyes, wide and bewildered, search the corners of the room, a little girl's eyes, but her mouth is suddenly resolute.

*

It's almost dark. Amy watches the last light falter along the distant hills. Behind them the sky, sullen with clouds, looks bruised. She darts across the road and starts to run. It feels good, running. As if she's a little girl again, running home. All those winter evenings after netball practice, she and Krystal running through the deserted streets, laughing and shouting. The wind whips her hair across her eyes and she pauses to push it back. For one breathless moment, she thinks she hears Krystal behind her. 'Go on. What are you stopping for?' and it's as if Krystal herself runs past her, her face dark and intense, her strong brown legs pumping furiously. Amy slows to a walk.

When she reaches her parents' house, she waits a moment before knocking. She wants to hold on to her memories. At last, biting her lip, she raises her hand.

Her little sister Narelle opens the front door. She flings herself into Amy's arms, her cheeks pink with excitement. 'Amy, Amy where's Timmy? You did bring Timmy, didn't you? You promised. You said next time I could play with him.'

Krystal pushes her out of the way. ''Course she didn't. You can see that. Stop carrying on.' She turns her attention to Amy and her expression changes.

A mask, thinks Amy despairing, her face is a mask and she has to clench her hands against the sudden lurching of her heart.

'What are you doing here?' says Krystal. 'You know what Dad said. He doesn't want you round here.'

'I came to see Mum.'

'Well, you'd better hurry up. He'll be home soon. You get him going, it'll be me and Narelle who'll suffer. You ought to think about that before you come flouncing round here like you own the place.'

'I don't…' Amy's voice falters but she meets her sister's eyes defiantly. Then, quickly, before Krystal can stop her, she's past her, into the front room, her arm around Narelle. 'I'll bring Timmy next time, Rellie. Or, tell you what, why don't you get Mum to bring you round to my place? Saturday. Saturday would be good. We'll be home then, some time Saturday afternoon.'

Narelle nods, her eyes round and solemn and Amy tightens her arm around her. 'Yes,' she whispers to herself. 'Saturday. Come Saturday,' and all the time something in her is crying out to Krystal, something only she can hear…her sister's name over and over again…Krystal who shares her earliest memories, Krystal who was once the other half of herself. But Krystal, with a toss of her head, has retreated to the other side of the room where she's got her schoolbooks spread out on the coffee table.

Amy finds her mother in the kitchen, busy at the stove. Amy leans against the doorframe and watches her until at last her mother turns and notices her.

'Amy, love. I didn't know you were here. You all right?'

'Yeah. I…I wondered if you could look after Timmy on Thursday. I've…I've made an appointment like you said. They'll do it then, early they said, but Timmy…'

''Course I'll have him. I said I would.'

'But Dad. What about Dad? He…'

'Oh, Amy, your dad'll be all right. He loves you. You know he does. All this, well, it's been a bit of a shock to him, you going off with Jason and the baby. He'll come round.' She wipes her hands on a tea towel and her mouth tightens. 'Don't you worry about your Dad. I can deal with him.'

Amy, her head down, runs one finger along the edge of the bench. 'You're not going to tell him about this, though, are you? Not about this, this other baby.'

'Oh, love.'

'And the girls. You won't tell them either, will you? Please, Mum. I couldn't bear…' Amy's eyes are wide and pleading and she clutches at the bench with both hands.

Her mother purses her mouth. 'I'm not telling anyone.' She turns back to the stove and carefully adjusts the gas jet under the soup. 'Jason's going with you, of course?'

'No. He doesn't think I should do it. He's gone back to his mother.'

'Amy…' Her mother takes a step or two toward her but Amy's head's up now and her mother stops, disconcerted.

'He'll come back. I know he will. And if he doesn't…' Amy's voice trails away uncertainly but the hardness is still in her face and her mother says quickly, placatingly, 'You'll be all right, love. After Thursday. Trust me. And you've got Timmy. That's what you've got to concentrate on. Timmy. Being a good mother to Timmy.'

'I know. I just…' Amy bites at her lip. 'I'd better get going. I promised Mrs Thomas I wouldn't be long. She's got Timmy. But I didn't want…I didn't want her to have him Thursday. I wanted you…'

'I know, love.' Amy's mother goes to her and puts her arm around her. 'It'll be all right, trust me.'

Amy grabs her mother's hand and holds it for a moment against her cheek, then, with a little incoherent cry, she pulls herself away.

Outside it's begun to rain. Amy shivers and pulls up the collar of her jacket. Then she sets her teeth and flings back her hair. Timmy, she thinks, Timmy. I've got to get back to Timmy. She slams the gate behind her and runs out into the street.

*

Amy wakes to the sound of Timmy's crying. She picks him up out of his cot and carries him into the kitchen so she can warm his bottle in a jug of hot water. It's almost morning. She takes him into the lounge and sinks down in the nearest chair. Light from the open doorway spills across the floor but it's quite dark where she's sitting. Amy's glad. The darkness is oddly comforting.

She puts the bottle in Timmy's mouth. Dawn is not far off. In front of her, the window is a pale square and she focuses all her attention on it.

Her arms tighten around the baby. 'Oh, Timmy,' she whispers. 'I didn't want to do it. I wanted to keep him. Both of you. I wanted both of you.' She's crying now. The tears slide down her cheeks but she makes no effort to brush them away. 'I had to. Oh, Timmy, I had to.'

Outside the first light quivers on the leaves of the creeper by the window. Amy catches her breath. She sits suddenly still, the baby asleep in her arms. At last she gets up and takes him back into the bedroom. Very gently she lays him down in his cot and tucks his blanket around him.

The Trail Bike

Dad's been working on the trail bike all morning. I get an old paint tin and sit down next to him. I like watching him. He's got special hands. It's not just that he can fix things. It's more than that. Like sometimes when I come home from school after everything's gone wrong, my Dad'll come and put his hands on my shoulders or maybe he'll tousle my hair and then everything's all right again. Neither of us says anything. We don't have to. His hands are enough. It's sort of like magic.

It's hot in the shed. Dad wipes his face with a bit of rag. 'Hand me that spanner over there, Bundy,' he says. 'Won't be long now. Bet you can hardly wait to try her out. Bike like this, it's every boy's dream. My dad, he thought it'd be a waste of money and of course there were the neighbours, noise and all that. Different out here, though. No one to care 'cept the sheep, and they'll soon get used to it. You'll be able to ride her all day. Sunup till sundown.'

My throat feels tight. I can't let myself meet his eyes. I don't like things that make a lot of noise.

Dad drops the spanner. He's grinning like Father Christmas. 'Hey, I reckon we've done it, mate. I reckon we've fixed her. Come on, Bundy boy. Let's try her out.'

We go outside. Dad kick starts the motor. It splutters and coughs a bit but then it roars into life. I grit my teeth and clamber on. I nearly fall but Dad steadies me and then I get my balance and I'm off. Dad runs alongside me, his face all red, and he's shouting and waving his hat in the air. The bike's going like crazy. The wind stings my eyes and I hold on tight and the corner of the paddock's coming up but I jerk the handlebars sideways so it's all right and I've got the rhythm now and it's like flying. Only...only...I've never wanted to fly. It's too fast. You'd never get to notice things.

Skye comes running out of the house. She's got on her plastic tiara and a long purple dress that used to be Mum's. When I whiz past her, she shouts out something. I can't hear her properly but I know what she wants anyway. I skid to a stop.

'Oh, Bundy, Bundy, let me have a go. Can I, Daddy? Can I?'

Dad shakes his head at her but I know he won't mind so I say, 'Come on then. Hurry up.'

Forgetting she's a princess, she hitches up her skirt and I help her on.

'Don't cry if you fall off,' I warn, but I know she won't. I only say it to sound big because I'm older.

Skye goes round two or three times before Dad makes her get off. You can tell she doesn't want to. I feel a bit sorry for her. I wish I could let her turn last all afternoon. But then Dad would be disappointed. I'm the boy. I'm the one he got the bike for.

So that's what we do. All afternoon. I ride the bike. Dad runs beside me. His face gets redder and redder. Skye waits by the gate. She's lost her crown and her dress is all torn down the front but she doesn't seem to have noticed. Every time I pass her, she cheers and claps. You can tell she's pretending I'm winning a race.

After a while, Mum comes out with Tansy balanced on her hip. Mum's face is all soft and dreamy and she's got her hair pulled back in a ponytail so she looks like a little girl. She's happy just watching. And I'm happy too. I don't much like riding the bike. I'd rather be sitting at the edge of the scrub watching the blue wrens at the septic overflow. But my Dad's gone to a lot of trouble. He's bought me the bike and he's spent all morning fixing it. I give him a quick grin and ride round the paddock one more time.

Birth of Sarah-Rose

Rain and a drift of falling leaves. I turn from the window frowning. Soon it will be winter. Someone…Shakespeare…'now is the winter of our discontent'…only it'll be worse than that, I know it will. Spring, a baby ought to be born in spring…new grass…the suddenly tender sky…

'Oh, Callum, Callum.' I stop and put my hand across my mouth. Months ago, when he left me, I promised myself I'd never say his name again.

I go with my father in the ute to a garage sale.

'We need a cot,' he says. 'Something for the baby to sleep in.'

'Don't they have baskets? They always do in books.'

'I asked Stephanie. She said she and Bruce would get you a pram. She's going into town next week. They've got a sale on at one of the department stores. She said to let her know if you wanted anything else.'

I say stubbornly, 'I'm sure we only need one of those basket things. We haven't got room for a cot.'

'Oh, Maja, love. Babies grow. In a few months…'

'Don't,' I say sharply. 'I don't want to think about it.'

He looks at me for a moment, his lips pursed, and I think he's going to say something but he just shakes his head and concentrates on his driving. I turn my head and stare out of the window.

After a while my father says, cautiously, 'I was talking to Stephanie on the phone last night. She said we could have her room for the baby. Would you like that, love? Do up her room a bit, paint it, get some new curtains. I thought it might be kind of fun, you and me, getting it ready.'

I look at my hands in my lap. My throat feels choked up. 'No,' I whisper. 'No.' He starts to protest and I struggle to explain. 'It's not because of the baby. I guess a room for it would be good, special, and it should have something special but that's Stephanie's room and I don't want…' I swallow and try again. 'I don't want to take it away from her. Not yet. If we change it, make it the baby's room, then it'll be like, it'll be like she doesn't belong to us any more, like she's…'

'Oh, Maja, sweetheart, Stephanie's got her own life now, her life with Bruce. She doesn't need…'

I lift my chin. 'The baby will make its own place,' I say. 'It'll have to because I'm not letting it take Stephanie's.'

I stop then. My feelings about my sister are so complicated. When I was little, after our mother died, she looked after me but then she married Bruce and it's like she left me. All of them – my mother, Stephanie, Callum – all of them have left me. In the end I wasn't enough so they left me. But still, Stephanie, she hasn't gone quite away. Sometimes it's like she's still there, like she hasn't quite forgotten…

I glance quickly at my father. He doesn't say anything but I don't know if that means he understands or not. I say, carefully, 'If we got rid of my desk, we could fit the cot in my room.'

My father nods. 'All right then.'

I reach over and put my hand on his knee. 'Later, when it's bigger, then we'll work out something else. And it's good of you to be thinking about a room for it.'

'I helped your mother. I helped her get ready for you and Stephanie. Why wouldn't I do the same now?'

Because, I think, because this isn't your child, this isn't anyone's child, it's here and we have to deal with it but it isn't as if anyone really wants it. I push my clenched hand into my mouth. I'm frightened. I'm frightened of my own whirling thoughts. My baby, my baby, but the baby struggling inside me doesn't seem to have much to do with me. It was a dream, I think desperately, a dream I made up when I thought Callum and I would always be together, our baby, spiky-haired with his little fat cheeks and his round dark eyes. He was something I made up just like I made up Callum loving me. And then, then Stephanie begging me to have a termination, 'You're so young, Maja, seventeen, only seventeen,' but 'No, no, can't you see, I love him, I don't want to but I do and I can't, I can't kill it.' If she asked me now, if it were possible now, I'd say…I'd say…

This baby's real. I don't want it to be but I can feel it. All the time now. Struggling. And it can feel me. It must be able to. My body holding it in, my body restricting it, stopping it from doing what it wants. My head starts to ache and I press my forehead against the closed window. The beginning of June, I think and then…and then…

The beginning of June and then at last it will be over.

*

The baby's got very quiet. I don't like it. I didn't like it when it moved all the time but it's worse now it's still.

*

Nights are the worst. I dream about Callum. I'm running along the path by the river…the lights are on at the cottage…

'Callum. Callum.' I'm in the doorway and he's holding me and laughing.

'Whatever's come over you, Maja? You're shaking. I told you I'd come back. I told you I'd come back for the baby.' He's holding me and my heart's beating so fast I can hardly breathe.

'But you said you didn't love me. You said…'

'Oh, Maja, you've made that up. You must have. Why would I say a thing like that? Aren't I here now? Aren't I holding you?'

But then he's gone. Instead of the cottage, a forest…pine trees… I can see their shadows across the snow. I stop and turn my head. There's men too. They've got long coats and hats that pull down over their ears and they shout to one another in thick, guttural voices. They're hunting a wolf. I saw it. I'm sure I saw it before, the memory of it's there in my mind, something dark among the trees. I start to run. They're hunting me too. All of them. The men. The wolf. Even the trees. They're waiting. They're waiting for me to fall and then they will be on me, all of them together.

Suddenly there's a shot. It explodes into splinters of light and I see the wolf, snarling, leap up to meet it. The men run forward, they're all around me, a circle of red, fierce faces and glittering eyes. They're shouting and laughing and waving their arms in the air and the wolf… The wolf… But I can't see the wolf any more. I'm lying in the snow clutching at my stomach and my hands are covered in blood.

'Please,' I whisper. 'Please.'

It isn't a dream. It can't be because I'm awake, I know I am, walls, ceiling, the pale square of my window, but the pain, the pain's still there and the men...in the shadows by the door, the men... Whimpering, I tighten my arms across my stomach. I have to protect the baby because the wolf, the wolf is leaping, and the men...

All at once I'm sitting up. There isn't a wolf. Or men either. It's the baby. It's the baby coming and there is nothing I can do to stop it.

Sobbing, I stumble out of bed and turn on the light.

*

My father drives me to the hospital. His hands, white-knuckled, grip the steering wheel and I turn my head away and stare out of the window.

The night's hazy with mist. Sky, paddocks, the road, they're all blotted out. Now and then I make out a clump of distorted gum trees. They reassure me. I press my hands against the glass and wish I were close enough to touch one.

I sigh. 'You don't have to stay with me when we get there, Dad,' I say. 'I'll be all right. First babies take a long time, twenty-four hours sometimes. You don't want to be stuck at the hospital all that time. I can get them to ring you when it's all over.'

'Maja...'

I don't hear the rest. Another pain's on me. They're a lot closer together. I clench my teeth and wait for it to subside. I'm getting used to them, though. As long as...just as long as they don't get much worse. I bite hard at the inside of my cheek until my mouth is full of the taste of blood. Twenty-four hours...if this goes on for twenty-four hours...

'Please,' I whisper. 'Please, Dad, I don't want you to stay at the hospital. I want to think of you safe at home by the fire with Mikki, with Sheepdog Mikki.'

'All right, love. Whatever you say.'

I take a deep breath. His kindness is almost too much. I go back to watching the road and the wavering mist. It's insidious, the mist, but it's beautiful too.

'What time is it?' I ask at last. The road seems interminable.

'Just after two. We're almost there.' He turns to me, his eyes anxious. 'You all right, Maja? You don't look so good.'

'I'm fine,' I say. 'Fine,' and I force my hands to keep still in my lap.

When we get there, I don't want to go in. The cabin of the ute seems suddenly safe, a place I'm used to, not like the hospital with its blazing lights. My father opens the door and reaches up to put his arms around me. 'Come on, love. You'll be all right. They'll tell you what to do.'

After a while I nod and let him lead me inside.

*

Afterwards, I don't remember. Not properly. Too much happens. A girl screaming, I remember a girl screaming. Or maybe it's a rabbit, a little helpless rabbit caught in a trap. I want to get up and rescue it but they won't let me. They've got a mask, a black mask, they hold it over my face. 'Breathe,' they say. 'Breathe through the mask.' I start to choke and they take it away.

Time gets mixed up. Hours. Minutes. Days. I stare at the white-faced clock on the wall, bewildered. 'Please,' I beg. 'Make it stop. Please,' and I think they give me another injection.

Then, suddenly, surprisingly, everything's back in focus. Lights. Faces. Eyes. In the corner a little plastic humidicrib. I'm very cold and I start to shiver but the pain's changed. It's easier now and I can bear it just as long as I do what they say. 'Push. Push with the pain, Maja,' and I close my eyes and concentrate and do what they want. I must be doing what they want because one of them, the short one with the glasses, wipes my face with a damp cloth and she's smiling. 'Just one more, dear. Come on, I can see the head. One more and it'll be over. Come on, dear. You're doing so well.'

I'm not sure what she means but I can't ask. I'm frightened to ask because the pain's back, it's worse, this has to be the worst and I feel my body gather itself together for one last desperate effort. I hear myself cry out. The pain explodes into a kaleidoscope of bright colours and a high, thin wailing. Spent, I open my eyes, dazed.

I look down. The one with the glasses is reaching for it, the baby. It's slippery with blood and mucus and I shudder at the sight of it. It's ugly. It's so ugly.

'Is it all right?' I whisper and the other one, the doctor, laughs and says, 'Of course she is. A little girl. You've got a lovely little girl.'

I look at it again. It's crying louder than ever and beating at the air with its fists. It's got a lot of wet bristly hair and its eyes are all squinched up and it's got puny thrusting legs and she's right, it's a girl. I turn my face away.

After a while they give her to me to hold. I want to refuse but I don't know how to tell them. The words, they're in my mind, I can hear them but though I open my mouth, I don't hear myself say them. They give her to me and she feels wrong, wet and slippery, and there's this smell about her, blood and something else, something animal and she's crying and I think, her mother, when is her mother coming, and all the time I know, I know and I start to shudder because I'm her mother, I know I'm her mother and I don't feel anything. Looking at her I don't feel anything at all. 'Please,' I whisper. 'Please…' and then they take her away and I feel myself sink down into the darkness and at last, after all these months, I'm free of her.

*

My father comes to see me. His face is very pink and he's got himself all dressed up in his best suit, he's even put a flower, a little white azalea, in his lapel. He smiles all over his face when he sees me. 'Maja,' he whispers. 'They said I couldn't stay long, only a few minutes. They said everything went very well but you have to rest, it took a lot out of you but, love, I am so glad to see you.'

I put my hand out to him. I want to cry. Just the sight of him. I want to cry like a little girl and I try to say something but the words all jam together in my throat and I can't.

He looks around him, frowning. 'I thought they'd have the little one in here with you. I thought I'd be able to see her.'

'This afternoon, I think they said. I don't remember. She's all right, though. I saw her.' I stop and turn my head away so he can't see my face. 'Dad, she's not much to look at. She's sort of ugly.'

'They all look a bit funny to begin with,' he says, laughing. 'I remember you and Stephanie. Not that I told your mother, mind. She was so proud.'

'I'm not...' I begin but suddenly it's too much of an effort and he understands because he takes my hand and he just sits there holding it. It's enough, though. I'm safe again. I close my eyes and fall back to sleep.

*

They bring me the baby to feed. She looks different. They've dressed her of course and parcelled her up in a striped blanket but it isn't that. Not entirely. She's drawn in on herself. Before, she was just born and she wasn't aware of anything. Now she is. She opens her eyes and stares at me. Her eyes are very dark, inky-blue, and they've got no depth or perhaps, perhaps it's the other way around and they've got too much. They stare at me without recognition and I catch my breath, disconcerted. She doesn't know who I am, she doesn't even want to know who I am and I thought...I thought, no matter how I felt, the baby would be different, it would know who I was and...and care.

I test the milk on the inside of my wrist like they show me and then I put the bottle to her mouth but she doesn't know what to do with it. She turns her head away and whimpers. I look up at the midwife.

'You should be feeding her yourself,' she says, her face stiff with disapproval. 'Healthy young woman like you. You should be ashamed.'

I turn my attention back to the baby. I jiggle the teat in her mouth and suddenly she takes hold and begins to suck and I sigh with relief.

*

Afternoon, or at least I think it's afternoon. I've been asleep again. I turn my head on the pillow. The light from the window slants across the polished floor and I hold my hands out to it. I splay my fingers and watch the light make the skin between them go translucent.

They've put the baby next to my bed in a little plastic cot. She makes snuffling noises in her sleep. A puppy, I think, a little abandoned puppy, Mikki when my father first found her in a sack by the side of the road with a lot of dead brothers and sisters. I bite down hard on my lip and go back to staring at my out-stretched hands.

Stephanie comes. Her heels beat out their own rhythm on the floor, brisk, purposeful, she's wearing her office clothes, her face is carefully made up, her hair, smooth and sleek; it swings against her shoulders like a fall of silk. I sigh. She's hiding, I think, she's been doing it for years and I wonder when it began, Stephanie being the efficient receptionist, the mature older sister, Bruce's wife, when what I need, what I want more than anything is the other Stephanie, the one'd who'd hurry home from school every afternoon to play with me, the one who held my hand at our mother's open door when she was dying and calling out our names.

I let her kiss me but when she starts to bend over the baby, I give my attention to the flowers she's brought.

'Oh, Maja,' she whispers, gathering the baby up in her arms. 'Oh, Maja, she's so sweet. Don't you think so? Don't you want to just…'

'You'll wake her up if you're not careful and she'll cry. You won't be so rapt then.'

'Don't be silly. She's a darling, a little darling.' She comes and sits on my bed and turns to me, bright-faced. 'What are you going to call her? I've been waiting all morning to find out. I asked Dad but he didn't know.'

I give a sudden start. A name. I'd forgotten she'd need a name. All those months I was pregnant and it never occurred to me the baby would have to have a name.

'I haven't decided yet.'

'Well, hurry up then. What sort of names do you like? Rebecca? Jessica? Sophie?' She giggles. 'Ermyntrude?'

I shake my head. 'I don't know. I haven't given it much thought.'

'Do you want me to bring you one of those name books? I could get one from the library. Or maybe…' Her expression changes. 'I thought maybe you could call her after Mum. Mary. Dad would like that. I know it's a bit old-fashioned but…'

My mouth goes dry. 'No. I don't want to name her after anyone. She should have a name of her own.'

It isn't true. I don't want the baby to have a name at all. It's all right the way things are. Her and me. Not the way it's supposed to be, of course, but good enough. A name will spoil it, get between us, it'll make her a person and then…then…

'She's too little to have a name,' I say desperately. 'In a week or two…'

But Stephanie's not listening. She's crooning over the baby, rocking her in her arms and the joy in her face spills over so it illuminates the baby as well as herself.

*

I don't like it in here. Nothing is real. I do what they tell me. I look after the baby. I feed her and change her and when she won't sleep, I sit on my bed and rock her. In the morning I take her down to the nursery and they show me how to bath her. She doesn't like that. She screams. She flings out a little star-fish hand and I feel my throat get tight because she's suddenly so defenceless. I wrap her quickly in the towel but my hands start to shake and my eyes prickle with tears.

It's not fair. She's so helpless and all she's got is me.

Tomorrow they are letting us go home.

'I don't know,' I tell her. 'I don't know whether that will be better or worse. You'll just have to trust me.'

Her eyes stare into mine. They haven't changed, I think, shuddering. They still see everything and yet…yet… She doesn't know…the whole world…Callum holding me in the darkness, his lips against my hair, 'Maja, Maja' and in the end it meant nothing, I meant nothing and so we are left, her and me, with nothing but one another and I know that it isn't enough, it's never going to be enough and in the end she'll know it too.

'I haven't even named you but I will,' I say, suddenly contrite. 'I'll think of something special so at least you'll have that and I'll try, I promise you, I'll try to do things right but I don't really think…'

I have to stop then because I'm crying, though I don't really know why.

Andrzej

He's not like other little boys. I don't know why. Perhaps it's the way he stands, rigid as a soldier. Or his clothes. And his hair, especially his hair. Lots of children have fair hair, of course. Blonde, my mother says. She says it wistfully, like it's a good thing to have. My hair's not blonde. It's brown. Light brown but brown all the same. The boy's hair is white, really white, and so thick it falls over his face so you can't see his eyes. You can see his mouth all right, though. It's too tight. I know what that means. He's frightened. He's trying not to cry.

Mrs Goldsworthy pushes him forward. 'Now, children,' she says, 'this is Andrew. He's come all the way from Poland. But he's Australian now, aren't you, Andrew? Australian like us.'

The little boy doesn't answer. I clench my hands in my lap. I wish I knew how to warn him. It's dangerous not to answer Mrs Goldsworthy. Especially when she sounds friendly. It's most dangerous of all not to answer her then.

Mrs Goldswothy shows Andrew his seat. It's the only empty one left, near the door next to Shirley. I feel sorry for him, having to sit next to Shirley. Shirley's mean. At her birthday party last week, she was rude to me. 'That isn't a proper present, Lily,' she said in front of everyone. 'You didn't buy it in a shop.' She was right. Mum made her a face-washer out of an old towel and decorated it with lazy daisy flowers and French knots. I thought it was pretty. I've got one of my own just like it, but of course Shirley has lots of pretty things. She even has a real doll.

Shirley drags her chair as far away from Andrew as possible. She probably thinks he's poor too. His clothes are so peculiar. I frown a bit. Little boys don't wear overalls to school. Overalls are for babies. Andrew's overalls are bright blue and he's got a red shirt. They're good colours, shouting for joy colours. It's funny how colours have feelings of their own. Like grey. Grey is a proper school colour. Most of the boys wear grey and even some of the girls, specially in winter when…

'Lily,' says Mrs Goldsworthy suddenly and I snap to attention. Mrs Goldsworthy doesn't say anything else but she picks up her ruler. Then she smiles. There is something wrong with her smile. She's got too many teeth.

I stumble to my feet. 'Yes, Mrs Goldsworthy.'

'Maybe you'd like to come out here and copy your spelling words onto the blackboard. Maybe that will help you concentrate.'

The blood rushes into my cheeks. Mrs Goldsworthy knows I get my letters all mixed up. She knows it makes the other children laugh. I go to the blackboard and pick up the chalk. Say. Hay. Away. It's a good page in the primer this week. Kathleen and Tom are at the farm. I like Kathleen and Tom and their little dog, Scottie. They have such fun. Last week they made a kite with a long tail decorated with twisted paper bows. A farm is better, though. There's a good picture of a horse too, a draught horse like Mr Lambert across the road has to pull the plough between his grapevines. Mum says he's too old-fashioned, he ought to get a tractor like Uncle Don. I'm glad he hasn't. A horse is real. Once, he let me have a ride on it and…

'Lily,' says Mrs Goldsworthy again.

Quickly I go on with my words. May. Fray. Ray… I'm lucky. None of them need the treacherous letter 'b'.

It rains at lunchtime so we can't go outside to play. We have to eat our sandwiches in the porch instead. I don't mind. Roslyn shares her biscuits with me. They're special nursery rhyme ones. I have Little Miss Muffet and Humpty Dumpty. Roslyn has Little Jack Horner and Simple Simon. They all taste the same. It's only the pictures that are different. When we've finished, Roslyn makes me tell her a story. The others listen too. I don't care. I like making up stories. Andrew stands at the door by himself. Jimmie goes over to him and tries to make friends but Andrew takes no notice. He doesn't even smile.

'I don't expect he understands English,' says Shirley, primming up her mouth. 'He's probably one of those refugees.'

My throat feels thick. I stare at her. 'But…but how can he come to school if he doesn't know what we're saying? How can he…?'

I glance over at Andrew but he turns his head away. I see his eyes, though. Underneath his hair. A quick glimpse. He has the bluest eyes I've ever seen. But that's all. You can't tell anything from them. Most people, most people look out at you from their eyes. Mum and Uncle Don and my sister Barbie. Even Shirley and Roslyn and that smart alec, Roger. Mrs Goldsworthy. Most of all Mrs Goldsworthy. Their eyes tell you who they are. But not Andrew. His eyes are secret. Only his mouth. That tells you he's brave. Probably just as brave as Daddy who went away to fight the Japanese before I was born and never came back because it was the war then and they killed him.

After lunch, Andrew runs away. I'm surprised. The worst part of the day's over. And Tuesday afternoon is plasticine. Mrs Goldsworthy finds an old lump for Andrew and lends him Sandra Regan's lino mat because Sandra's away and doesn't need it. But Andrew won't play with the plasticine. He just sits there staring at it. Jimmie leans across the aisle and nudges him. He holds out the aeroplane he's made so Andrew can see what to do but Andrew won't look. He just gets up and walks out of the door.

Mrs Goldsworthy's cheeks go red. She lunges after him, slamming the door behind her. After a few minutes, Andrew screams. A jumble of words burst from him. They're like bullets. They splinter the air.

Shirley turns round. 'Told you,' she hisses. 'Told you. That's Polish. He can't speak English.'

Mrs Goldsworthy drags Andrew back inside. She's won. I clench my hands in my lap. She marches over to the cupboard and wrenches open its door. She pulls out a piece of white cord. It writhes and twists but Mrs Goldsworthy knows how to make it do what she wants. She jerks Andrew's arms behind him and ties his wrists together. Then she forces him down on his chair. When she's used up all the cord, she begins again with another piece. At last she's done and she straightens up. None of us move.

Her eyes sweep over the classroom and she nods, satisfied. 'I'm sorry I had to do this to you, Andrew,' she says. Her lips stretch into a smile. 'But you have to learn how to behave. We don't run away from school, do we children? Not here in Australia. We sit quietly at our desks and do as we are told.'

I feel sick. Mrs.Goldsworthy has put Andrew's chair in the front so we can all see him. He isn't crying, though. I drop my head and look at my hands in my lap. That's what makes it so bad. Andrew isn't crying. We've done all this to him but he still won't let himself cry.

Robbie

There's a boy at school, he's younger than us, so he's only in Grade Four, and he hasn't got any hands, just stumps at the end of his arms. The skin there is very pink and stretched, as if there isn't really enough of it, but apart from that he seems quite ordinary.

All boys are the same, especially little ones. They push and shove and jump around shrieking.

'Nuisances,' says Talia, wrinkling up her nose. 'They ought to be kept in the zoo.'

Everyone laughs then.

Except Amber-Louise. She's obsessed with the boy with no hands. Whenever she sees him, her face goes white and sick and she shudders. 'Oh, it's disgusting,' she says. 'I can't bear to look at him.'

'Don't then,' I say. 'No one's making you.'

Amber-Louise flushes but she pouts up her mouth too so Wendy puts a protective arm around her. 'Don't listen to Jess,' she says. 'She's in one of her moods.'

'I'm not,' I say. 'I just think…' but I don't go on.

No one's interested in my opinion so I give up and stalk into the classroom by myself.

Later, though, Amber-Louise seeks me out. She's always doing that, trying to be friends. I don't know why. I've always hung around by myself. That's the way I like it.

Amber-Louise puts her hand on my arm. 'Come to the library with me, Jess. I'm late with my book report. I thought p'raps you could help me find a book, an easy one.' She smiles winningly. 'You're always reading. You must have read all the books they've got by now.'

I glance at her quickly in case she's trying to take the mickey but her eyes are kitten-blue and innocent. 'All right.'

I follow her across the quadrangle and past the shelter shed where a crowd of little boys are playing on the old basketball court.

'There's that boy again,' says Amber-Louise, stopping. 'Do you know what he's called, Jess? Do you know his name?'

'No and I don't care. He's nothing to do...'

But Amber-Louise goes on as if I haven't spoken. 'Robbie. His name's Robbie. I asked one of the other boys. And I know how he writes too. He holds his pen between those stumps of his and...'

I've had enough. 'Look, are you coming to the library or not because...'

Amber-Louise's voice drops and she clutches at my arm. 'Jess, what do you think happened to his hands? Do you think he was born like that or p'raps something happened afterwards and...'

I pull my arm away. 'Amber-Louise, I told you...'

'Mum's having a baby,' says Amber-Louise before I can finish. 'She's always wanted one, ever since she had me and now it's happened.' Her face changes suddenly and her lips quiver.

I'm shocked. For once she isn't pretending. The fear in her face is real.

'Last night,' she whispers. 'Last night I dreamt about the baby. Mum was in the hospital because he'd just been born. She had him all wrapped up in a blue bunny rug and when she pulled it back to show him to me, I saw... Oh, Jess, he didn't have any hands. He was like Robbie. My little baby brother and he was just like Robbie.'

'That's stupid,' I say. 'Really stupid, Amber-Louise. Of course nothing's going to happen to your brother. Robbie must have been in an accident, a car accident probably because...'

'Yes,' says Amber-Louise lifting her head and meeting my eyes. 'Yes. But you don't know, Jess. You don't know what's going to happen. No one does. Even if he's born all right, then...then...'

Her eyes go wide and dark and they look beyond me and I feel myself start to shudder because she's right. We don't know. Tomorrow or the next day anything could happen and... My mother. A long time ago, my mother got sick and she went away and she hasn't come back and even if my father knows why it happened, why Mum stopped talking and laughing and being herself, even if he knows, he doesn't know how to make her better any more than the doctors in the hospital where she has to stay. And Robbie...whatever happened to him, they couldn't stop it and now he hasn't any hands and there's all the other things, wars and people starving and…

I swallow hard and turn back to Amber-Louise. 'Stop it,' I whisper. 'Stop going on about that boy. I keep telling you. I don't want to hear about him.'

Amber-Louise purses up her lips and starts to smooth down her skirt. Her hands are narrow and white, she's got long tapering fingers and her nails are pink and translucent like the inside of a very old shell. They aren't like little girl's hands at all.

She says, her voice flat and expressionless as if she's reciting a lesson, 'My mother says that boy shouldn't be allowed to come to school with us. He's deformed. He should go to a special school where we don't have to see him. That's what Mum says.' Her head jerks up and she meets my eyes defiantly. 'I think that too. He's ugly. If we didn't have to see him, we wouldn't have to think about him and…and other things.' She pauses a moment and then her voice seems to break so I can hardly hear her. 'I don't like ugly things. I wish… Oh, Jess, don't you wish things were always…'

'Yes,' I say before I can stop myself. 'Yes, I wish…' and I close my eyes quickly and bite at my lip because the feelings inside me are suddenly too much for me.

More than anything, I want my mother to come home. My father and I'd be whole again then. A family. Instead, we're broken. I open my eyes and look at Amber-Louise and I think, if she knew, if Amber-Louise knew about my mother, she'd say we were ugly too, not from spitefulness, not that, but because we aren't the way we're supposed to be anymore than Robbie is.

'Things are ugly,' I say. 'All sorts of things and you might as well get used to it, Amber-Louise, because it isn't ever going to be any different. You have to…' I hesitate but the words come out anyway, fierce and proud, though that's not how they sounded in my mind. 'You just have to bear it.'

I turn my attention quickly to the boys on the court. The ball they're playing with bounces in front of us and Robbie leaps forward to grab it. He cradles it in his arms and then, graceful as a ballet dancer, he spins around and hurls it through the hoop.

I glance over at Amber-Louise. She's watching them too. Her cheeks are flushed and she's twisting her hands awkwardly together. It's like I'm seeing her for the first time. It's like somehow we've become allies.

'Come on, Amber-Louise,' I say softly. 'We'd better hurry if we're going to get you that book.'

For a moment, Amber-Louise doesn't move. Then she links her arm through mine and we go over to the library and up the steps together.

The Bear

Last night I dreamt about Emily. I don't want to think about it. It's ridiculous. Emily is just a little girl, one of fourteen in my Grade Three class.

Today, to punish myself, I wouldn't let myself look at her. Oh, I marked her work as usual but when the children were busy with their projects, I wouldn't let myself glance in her direction. I never realised till then how often I do. It's frightening.

*

Yesterday, I over-reacted.

All sorts of people are sensitive to beauty. A rose. A bird in flight. The sky prickled over with stars. A little girl's face. For centuries, poets and painters have celebrated such things. They speak for all of us.

And a schoolteacher. In his lifetime, he becomes a connoisseur of children's faces. He'd have to be blind otherwise.

So there's no harm in it

Sara Jennings has wild red hair.

Billy Saunders has the widest, bluest eyes.

Emily Morris is the prettiest little girl I have ever seen.

Nothing sinister in any of that. Just observations.

And my dream. What of it? Probably brought about by indigestion. I had mushrooms in rich cream sauce for supper. In any case, I'm not responsible for what I dream.

*

I've found out more about Emily. It's important for a teacher to know what kind of homes the children come from. Graeme McLeod's aggression is easily understood once you realise he has a drunken stepfather.

I imagined that a child like Emily would come from an upper middle-class family, a doctor's daughter perhaps. There's something delicately bred about her, a gazelle; all her movements are so graceful and her eyes…

But I was wrong. Emily's mother runs a disreputable boarding house the other side of town and no one seems to know who her father is. I can hardly believe it. A little girl like her.

*

I have been watching the children. Discreetly, of course. It would never do for them to catch me staring at them. The other little girls seem to avoid Emily. I used to think it was because of her shyness. Now I wonder if it isn't some kind of prejudice. I've seen Sara Jennings looking at her and then whispering to Natalie Crawford. Then they both giggle.

I think I will keep my notes about Emily in a special book. After school, I called in at the newsagents where I found what I was after – a leather-bound journal with thick, gilt-edged pages. I even bought a new fountain pen, one that I'll keep just for writing about her. Maybe I'll get her name embossed on the front cover. I haven't quite decided.

I feel restless, excited. I want to start writing immediately but I can't concentrate. The book is full of empty pages and I turn them carefully. My heart is beating very fast. Tomorrow. Tomorrow, I promise myself, tomorrow I'll let myself start.

*

We're organising the school concert. I didn't choose Sara for the princess though it was obvious that's what she expected. I didn't choose Emily either. How could I? Emily is mine. I don't want other people to notice her.

*

I'm used to the dreams by now so I don't let them worry me. Sometimes, remembering them in the classroom, I go hot with embarrassment. I'm careful never to touch Emily, not even accidentally when I'm marking her work. She's only a little girl. She'd be frightened if she knew how strongly I feel about her. Not that there's anything wrong in it. I'm sure of that.

Sometimes I think she knows, knows that I… It's so hard to write, though why it should be I don't quite know. I love her. There, I've admitted it.

When I look at my words on the page, I start to tremble. I can't help it.

I know Emily so well. I know things about her no one else does. The way her hair grows around her ears. The exact colour of her eyes, smoky-grey, like the sky in the morning before the light makes it go blue. Other things. More important things. How timid she is, how bewildered…

I wish I could adopt her. No one will ever love her like I do so she should belong to me.

I don't like thinking about those men at her mother's boarding house. But I can't help it. I think about them all the time. They look at her. They look at her when she's eating her meals or watching television or playing in the garden. They can look at her whenever they want.

*

It's not enough to watch Emily and write about her. I need something of hers to keep.

Of course, if I were to ask, she'd give me something, a handkerchief perhaps or… But I can't do that. She might tell her mother. That would be dangerous. People are so suspicious. They distort things.

Last night I had an idea.

This afternoon I got the children to draw pictures. We are meant to have Art once a week so it wasn't anything unusual.

I don't like deceiving the children but it's the only way. I'm going to tell them I lost their drawings. I don't expect they'll mind especially as I'll let them draw another lot next Thursday. I might even organise a bit of a competition – prizes for the best one, that sort of thing.

Emily's picture is in front of me now. It's a group of dolphins. The mother dolphin is leaping right out of the water. She's smiling. I hadn't expected Emily to draw such a happy picture. Lately, in the classroom, I've thought she looked rather sad.

I've written on the back of her picture. I shouldn't have really. But

I know she wouldn't mind. I put, 'To Mr Robbins from Emily.' I didn't deliberately copy her writing but it turned out like that anyway.

I wanted to write 'Love, Emily' but I wouldn't let myself. It wouldn't be honest. Emily'd never write that. She's too young. She doesn't know anything about love, especially not a love like mine.

*

I have started buying things for Emily. I know it's foolish because I won't ever be able to give them to her. But I can keep them for her as a sort of trust.

At first I got little things. A string of glass beads. A gauze butterfly. A lead-light bird. Today I bought her a porcelain doll. It was very expensive but I knew, the moment I saw it, that I had to get it for her. It's exquisite – hand-embroidered dress and bonnet, little lace pantalets, a fall of blonde curls tied with blue ribbon. And such a sweet face – delicate pink cheeks, a little rosebud mouth, wide dark-lashed eyes. I think it was the eyes that made me get it. They are so like Emily's own.

All evening I've felt like a parent the night before Christmas, anticipating her delight. Finally I wrapped it up and put it with her other presents. They're in a cupboard in the spare room. I don't know where else to keep them.

*

After the children left today, I found Emily's hair ribbon on the floor. It had fallen down by her desk. Someone had even trodden on it. It was creased and dirty but oh! so precious. So much more than an ordinary red ribbon. I've put it in my book as a keepsake. The only thing of hers I have. The only thing of hers I will ever have. The dolphin picture doesn't count any more. A ribbon is so much more personal. This morning it tied back her hair and now it's mine. I can't help myself. I pick it up and hold it against my lips.

Emily's hair is so pretty. Light brown. It falls down her back, curling slightly at the ends. I wish just once I could touch it…could…

There isn't anything wrong in thinking such things. Emily is a little girl and I love her. I would never hurt her. I would give her back her ribbon if I thought she would mind my having it. I would give it back at once. I wouldn't even feel sorry because the way she feels is more important than the way I do.

*

Emily is like a flower. Those lines from Shakespeare – 'How with this rage shall beauty hold a plea / Whose action is no stronger than a flower.' I remembered them suddenly this evening when I was about to write in my book. I got up and went over to the window. The evening sky was so soft and sweet but, even as I watched, the darkness came and filled my garden with shadows.

*

Last night in my dream Emily let me play with her hair. She put her arms around my neck and kissed me. Her hair smelt of flowers.

*

On my way back from the post office, I saw Emily in the park with one of the men from her mother's boarding house, the young one I've often noticed hanging round the pub. He was pushing Emily on the swing. She had her head tipped back and she was laughing.

For a moment I thought my heart had stopped. Her little laughing face. The sun on her hair. And the man's hands, his hands on the back of her dress, pushing her. I shut my eyes and made myself take deep breaths until I was calm enough to go on.

When I got home, I tried to read but I couldn't concentrate. I keep thinking about the man. I don't trust him. I don't trust him at all.

*

It is dark. Midnight. I can hardly write. But I must. I must. I must write it all down because otherwise…otherwise…

I was asleep. Dreaming. Emily and I were wandering through a forest of pine trees. The wind was mournful in the trees but Emily and I were happy. Light-hearted. She was running ahead of me laughing…there were blue and yellow flowers growing by the side of the path and every now and then she'd stop and pick a few. Her curls were tied back with scarlet ribbon, just like the one in my book. Suddenly a bear appeared. It seemed harmless enough, lumbering along among the bushes. Emily ignored it. She began to sing. At the sound of her voice, the bear rose up on its hindquarters. Horrified, I saw it had the face of a man. I knew what he wanted so I raced forward, heart pounding, but I was too late. He had hold of her. Her hair spilled over his arm. Brown silk, it shone like brown silk in the sun. I screamed. Or maybe it was Emily. I don't know.

There was nothing I could do. I couldn't move. I was paralysed, completely paralysed and I had to watch as he took her away though I knew what he would do to her the moment he had her to himself.

*

I haven't written in here for more than a month. I feel so many things but I know I can't write them down. I'm frightened. I'm frightened for Emily. Something bad is going to happen to her and I don't know how I can save her.

*

I picked a bunch of snowdrops today. I've put them in a vase on my desk. I keep looking at them as I write. I reach over and touch one. Bells. They're like little white bells. Emily, I think, Emily. Everything I look at, everything sweet and pure and gentle, everything is Emily.

*

It's obvious, though.

It's obvious what I have to do. I stare at the words I've written. All at once I put my hands over my face and start to sob. It's too much. What I have to do is too much.

But it's the only way. I know it is. It's the only way I can save her.

102

*

I can't wait much longer. I know I can't. If I do, it will be too late.

*

I saw Emily in the park again with the man. This time they had a little dog with them, a little white dog. The man gave Emily a ball and she stopped and threw it for the dog to chase. I tried to call out to her, to warn her, but my voice stuck in my throat so in the end all I could do was turn and hurry home.

*

I have to. Otherwise…the young man in the park…otherwise, the young man in the park will… Emily likes him. I could see she likes him and… I have no choice. It's as simple as that. I have no choice.

*

I've stolen a day. I didn't mean to but when I woke up I knew. Today. It was like someone had told me. Today is the day. My last chance. I'm so glad it's Saturday, the children's day.

I found Emily walking by the shops not far from where she lives. I stopped the car and called out to her. 'Emily, I've just been to see your mother. She said I could take you to the zoo today as a special treat because you did so well in your spelling test yesterday.'

Emily nodded. She didn't say anything but she climbed in beside me. She sat very straight, her eyes on the road ahead, her hands folded primly in her lap. Everything she does has such dignity. She knew on this last day exactly how I wanted her to behave. My little lady Emily.

Even at the zoo she was circumspect. Her eyes grew big and dark as I showed her the various animals but she didn't shout or laugh or run about like the other children. She always remembered who she was.

When we walked past the bears, though, she became a little girl again. She slipped her hand in mine. I could feel it trembling.

'I've always been frightened of bears,' she whispered.

I stopped in the middle of the path and knelt beside her. I held her so close I could feel the very delicacy of her bones. A bird, I thought, my Emily is a little, wild bird.

Then she said, 'Do you think, Mr Robbins, do you think I ought to be brave and look at them?'

My throat choked up but I managed to make my voice sound normal. 'Of course not. I don't like them either. Let's go and look at the giraffe.'

When we got tired, we sat in the sun and ate the sandwiches that I had bought at the kiosk. It was difficult deciding which animals we liked best.

Emily liked the antelope. 'And the peacock,' she added thoughtfully, throwing a handful of crumbs to the sparrows. 'Don't you like the way he puts his tail up and struts around, Mr Robbins?'

'Well, he's a bit ostentatious for me,' I said and offered her another sandwich. 'What about the bush-babies or the koalas?'

'They're nice,' Emily admitted. 'You feel you'd like to cuddle them. But,' she shook her head, 'they're not elegant. I like things to be elegant.'

I wanted to laugh; her face looked so serious. All at once she bent forward to pull up her socks and her hair parted, exposing the back of her neck.

I felt my mouth go dry and I jumped up. 'We haven't seen the elephant yet, Emily,' I said. 'Let's buy some peanuts and feed the elephant.'

Afterwards I took her to my place and showed her my garden. The first roses were out, the pale pink ones that are my favourites. I picked a bunch for her and we took them inside together. Then I led her into the lounge where I'd put her presents out ready. 'Look,' I said softly. 'Look what I've got for you.'

It was like I'd always imagined, Emily opening her presents, her eyes like stars. She sat on the floor, wrapping paper all around her, with her doll in her lap, crooning over it. Her hair fell like a curtain over her face and I caught my breath because I knew what I had to do.

*

I feel so confused. I thought…Emily and I… I thought that when I, when I… A consummation. I thought it would be a consummation.

104

I've put Emily on the couch. Her head lolls to one side and her mouth has gone slack. She doesn't look like Emily any more. She looks like a broken doll.

I don't know what to do.

I feel cheated.

It wasn't meant to be like this. It wasn't meant to be like this at all.

*

I fell asleep. I didn't mean to. I'd lighted a candle and put it on my desk next to my book so I could keep vigil. The shadows were so kind. They were kind to both of us. All I could see of Emily was her bright hair and one delicate, drooping hand.

But some time in the night the candle must have gone out and I fell asleep. I found myself dreaming again. Emily and I were in the forest. She was holding my hand like before and there were flowers in her hair, the little blue and yellow ones that grew by the path. When the bear came, I felt her hand tremble in mine so I said quickly, 'It's all right, Emily. He can't hurt you. I won't let him.' The bear rose up, snarling, on his hindquarters. 'You can't have her,' I shouted. 'She's mine. Emily is mine.' I put both my arms around her and hid her face against my coat.

The bear laughed then and reached for her. Suddenly my mouth went dry. The bear had my face. I felt my arms let go of Emily. My face. All the time the bear had my face.

*

I've lit the candle again but it doesn't help.

I know what I've done.

I was trying to save her. All the time I thought I was saving her... and...and...

Dawn has come. I stand by the window watching. The police will be here soon. I rang them. There was nothing else to do. When they come I'll tell them the truth. 'I am the bear,' I will say. I won't have to say anything else. That will be enough.

I am the bear.

105

Fulham Cove

On her way back from the shops, Molly takes the short cut through the railway station. The platform's deserted so Molly hauls her basket onto the waiting-room seat and sinks down next to it. The cement walls are pockmarked with graffiti and her eyes flick towards them automatically. 'Ryan 4 Shari'. 'James loves Tameeka'. 'For a good time ring Darice'. Molly likes the sound of their names. She can imagine the girls they belong to. Tall, elegant, they stand nonchalantly at street corners, watching the world through narrowed eyes. They put their hands up to their faces and flick at their hair. They know who they are.

Molly isn't much of a name. It's too old-fashioned. Childish. The sort of name you'd give a rag doll. Molly grimaces and gets up to examine the fly-specked timetable behind her. The names of the stations are almost like poetry. Acacia Park, Butterworth, Hove, Seaview, Seaview Downs, Fulham Cove. She stops then. Fulham Cove. Years ago, before Dad left, they'd had a holiday place at Fulham Cove. They'd gone there every summer. Behind the shack there was a bedraggled clump of tamarisk trees and she'd made herself a cubby there, a piece of rusty iron and an old box, and she'd played there every afternoon, waiting for it to be cool enough to go down to the beach.

Molly takes a deep breath. Her mind is a sudden kaleidoscope of forgotten images. Cliffs and spindrift and crying gulls. A handful of pink shells. Her little sister's footprints, an uneven stagger in the wet sand. Louise herself, digging, splashing, laughing, her cheeks red with excitement, her hair a tangle of curls. Molly's throat feels tight and she clenches her hands. She's not sure she wants to remember but now she's started she can't stop.

Louise's bucket full of little rock crabs. Her mother was angry then. 'Spiders,' she'd shouted. 'They look like spiders. Take them back to the beach, Paul. Take them back at once!'

One afternoon there was a summer storm and her father caught her up in his arms to reassure her. 'Sea-horses. Look, Molly, look at the white, tossing manes of the sea-horses.'

Her father. Molly feels her heart turn over and she grabs up her basket and stumbles down the station ramp. The images won't stop, though. A picnic on the beach, cucumber sandwiches gritty with sand and the fire her father made from driftwood. The flames leapt up blue and turquoise and green, sea-flowers, her father said. Molly can see suddenly his lean brown face, his hands; he had long, thin hands, her father, delicate, not like a man's hands at all.

And then the last holiday. Molly shuts her eyes for a moment and shudders. It's like she's back there, a little girl, six, seven, she can't quite remember. Her father's standing at the edge of the cliff staring at the sea. It's evening. The light has almost gone from the sky so the water's iridescent, silver, but the shadows of the rocks are already black across the sand. Molly runs up to him. Her mother's sent her to fetch him but when she reaches him, his face is so strange she hesitates, suddenly uncertain. It's only for a moment, though. He turns and sees her, calls out her name, swings her up in his arms, laughing and it's all right, he's familiar again. Only…only…it's not long after that that he leaves. Molly presses her lips together and walks faster.

She's come to a decision, though. She's catching the train this afternoon to Fulham Cove. Her mother won't like it. She doesn't like Molly doing things by herself. So far it hasn't mattered; Molly's been complaisant. She wrinkles her nose as the word comes into her mind. It's a rag doll word like her name. But this is different. She lifts her chin and stares ahead, suddenly resolute.

When she gets home, her mother's in the kitchen, stirring apricot jam on the stove. She looks up when she hears Molly at the door and her mouth goes tight. 'What took you so long? I told you I wanted that sugar in a hurry.'

'I'm sorry. I…'

But her mother's turned back to the jam so Molly sets the basket on the table and starts to unpack it.

When she's finished, she clenches her hands and says hesitantly, 'The holidays are nearly over. I thought if you didn't need me, I could catch the train to Fulham Cove. I could take Louise too. We could have a bit of a picnic. It wouldn't cost much, I'm sure, and...'

Her mother's head jerks up. 'Fulham Cove? What d'you want to go there for?'

'Just to see. We used to go there a lot, didn't we, when I was little? I'd just, you know, like to see it again.'

'Waste of time. Still, that'd mean nothing to you. Beats me. Fifteen and no more sense of responsibility than a child. You'd think by now you'd have grown up a bit, got a bit of sense. Oh well, go if you like. I don't care. You're no use here.' Then she whirls around, her eyes dark and dangerous. 'You're not taking Louise, though. I won't have you giving her ideas, telling her things that are best forgotten. Louise is staying right here with me.'

'I just thought she'd like it. Something different.' Molly swallows and begins again. 'Sandwiches. I thought I'd make some sandwiches and...'

'I'm not stopping you. There's plenty of tomatoes. Use some of them.'

Molly grimaces. She'd almost rather have plain bread and butter but her mother's watching her so she gets some tomatoes from the fridge and starts slicing them.

'You can't swim there,' her mother says suddenly, her eyes still on Molly. 'You do know that, don't you? It isn't safe. I won't have you swimming there.' Her voice starts to rise. 'Molly, you hear me? No swimming.'

'I wasn't going to. I just want to look and...'

'Can't think why. There's nothing there. Just rocks. Not like a proper beach. I never understood what your father saw in it. Nobody around. Just farms and a few fishermen. He wanted us to live there. In that shack. No electricity. No running water. And me with you two. I asked him. Time and time again, I asked him. Whatever for? He'd never answer.' She looks sharply at Molly. 'Like you, he was. Always mooning around, always wasting time.'

Molly bites at her lip and doesn't answer. There's nothing to say. A shield, her silence is a shield. She says it to herself in her mind and watches her hands wrapping up her sandwiches. Her heart starts to beat very fast. It's beating out a rhythm of its own. 'Fulham Cove. Fulham Cove. I'm going to Fulham Cove.' She hears it in her blood and she knows, she knows why her father wanted to live there, and it's wild and sweet, this knowing, and she struggles to hide it from her mother. She bends over her sandwiches, her hands busy with them, and her hair falls forward and hides her face and she knows she's safe again.

'I'll be back by six. I promise. Earlier if I can. I'm not sure of the trains but I think there's one at about five. And when I get back, I'll get the tea for you and clear up. You'll be tired then from the jam, it's so hot. You'll be able to have a bit of a rest.'

The danger's over. Her mother's shoulders slump wearily and she turns back to the stove. 'Yes. That'd be nice.'

Molly hesitates. All at once she wants to run to her mother, put her arms around her, tell her… But she can't. She knows she can't. Her mother 's not like other mothers. The girls at school, their mothers are friendly, they laugh and you can tell them anything, anything at all and they listen, they reach out their hands to casually touch their daughters' faces and their daughters, their daughters…

Very carefully, Molly puts her sandwiches in a bag. Then she goes to the door and, closing it quietly behind her, sets out, frowning, for the railway station.

Once on the train, though, her excitement comes back. Fulham Cove. Fulham Cove. She sings it softly to herself while she watches the suburbs give way to open countryside, paddocks and sheep, clumps of gum trees. She laughs aloud and then, embarrassed, puts her hand over her mouth. In the distance a horse is silhouetted for a moment against the sky, a horse running, its head proudly up, its plumed tail like a banner.

And then the sea. All at once she's six years old again, bouncing up and down in her seat. 'Look, Daddy. Look, the sea.' She can see his face, smiling, as he half turns toward her and her heart lurches again. She grips the windowsill with both hands and presses her face against the glass. At last the train jolts to a stop and she scrambles to her feet.

The station's smaller than she expected. There's not even a waiting room, just a battered, lopsided sign. 'Enough, though,' she says aloud but her smile wavers and she turns quickly and starts along the cliff path to the cove.

Below her, the sea hurls itself against the rocks, sending up spray white as mermaids' hair. Molly closes her eyes for a moment and takes it into herself. The sea's alive, relentless, and in the end it will win. Despite the fragility of its mermaids' hair, in the end the sea will win.

Downhill and all at once the cove. Molly catches her breath and runs towards it. Wind and the smell of salt, magic of sun on blue water, the sweet, white sand and in the distance a man and a boy scrambling over the rocks. Molly hears herself call out and she wrenches off her sneakers and flings them aside with her sandwiches. She stops, breathless, when she reaches the water, water edged with a lace of foam and so transparent she can see in it a school of tiny darting fish. Far out on the horizon there's a darker line of blue and above it the endless, endless sky. She feels something inside her give way and she whirls around laughing until, dizzy, she falls in a heap on the damp sand. When she gets up, she feels different. It's as if she's stopped being herself, has become instead part of the sea and sky and sand. She's one of the circling gulls, she's drifting with the water, she's a shell, a piece of sea-glass, a darting silver fish. She's free at last from the burden of herself.

Slowly, she starts to walk along the water's edge. In places, the sand has been washed away and the rock underneath is pink and yellow, scored by little ridges and cracks, but in other places it's smooth and polished like marble. Fascinated, she stops to kneel by a rock pool. She watches the wavering tentacles of the trapped sea plants and when her own hair, damp with spray, falls over her face she laughs aloud, it seems so much like another kind of seaweed. Later, she finds herself tracing, with infinite tenderness, the spiral of a broken shell. As she starts round the other side of the cove, she sees that the rocks close to the water are encrusted with periwinkles. They are round and black and shiny and she stops to touch them. They give to the light but the rocks, dark purple, take the light greedily back into themselves.

She squats down on a ledge of rock and thrusts both hands into the water. They look like sea creatures, pink and distorted, and she smiles to herself. She closes her eyes and lets her mind fill with images that splinter like light, a shard of broken shell, a discarded shark's egg, its leather petals curled like a rose, a trail of silver bubbles. And always, always the bright water flinging itself in triumph above the dark rocks.

Laughing, Molly jumps up and scrambles back to the sand. She's reached the end of the cove. Ahead of her, the cliffs jut into the sea and she can't go any further. She stands there staring at them, confused. All at once she's herself again. The skin of her face is tight with sunburn and when she licks her lips they're cracked and taste of blood. She shudders but it's all right. She's different, she knows she is, but it's all right.

'I've stretched,' she whispers looking up into the sky. 'In one afternoon, I've stretched. It's like…like the world's got bigger and I…I've got bigger too to fit.' She catches her breath and looks around her again. 'A shift in perspective,' she says and she likes the sound of the words because they somehow belong to the gaunt cliffs, the smudged horizon, the endless curving sky. The other things, the loss of her father, her mother's moods, her little sister, they stop mattering, she's not defined by them any more. 'I'm this,' she says, spreading wide her hands. 'I'm this as well.'

She turns and starts walking back along the beach. It's late, she knows it is, the light on the water's changed, it's softer, almost opaque. When at last she reaches the cliff path, she grabs up her sneakers and starts to run. She's suddenly afraid she will miss the last train. She promised her mother she would be home by six but she's sure it's past that already and the last train… 'I'm sorry, Mum' she whispers, clenching her hands. 'I'm sorry. I couldn't help it,' but she knows there is no way she can make her mother understand

her father perhaps, but her father left them years ago and she doesn't know where he is. 'But I could find him.' She stops, appalled. Her mother would be so angry but 'He's my father.' Her lips quiver and she turns her head away.

Behind her, the sea's like polished glass and, out of the new strength inside her, she cries out to it. 'I have to. I have to do this for myself. I have to do what's right for me.' The enormity of what she's said swirls around her. 'Spindrift,' she whispers. 'Spindrift,' and the word explodes in her mind in all its beauty and she starts to run again towards the station and the waiting train.

Sylvia

It's quite dark when I get off the train. I'm surprised. I hadn't thought the journey had taken that long. It's cold too. I pull up the collar of my jacket and fumble in my pocket for my cigarettes. I watch the train pull out of the station and disappear into the distance. Then I look around me but the station's quite deserted. The wind catches up an empty crisp packet and whirls it round idly before it discards it again. Frowning, I throw my cigarette butt onto the railway lines and pick up my bag.

I'm not sure how to get to my uncle's cottage. I'm not even sure why I've come. I got the letter from the solicitor almost a month ago. Until then, I hadn't known my uncle had died or that he'd left me his cottage. I hadn't seen him for years, not since I was a boy of nine and my mother left me with him for the summer. She and my father were having difficulties, she said; they needed to spend time without me. I didn't ask her what she meant. I was too angry. I concentrated instead on hating them, all of them, my mother, my father and my uncle. 'You'll like it there, at the beach,' my mother said, pleading, but all the way down on the train, I turned my head away and wouldn't look at her.

I stumble down the ramp from the railway station. I'd forgotten that time. Or I thought I had. My mind is suddenly full of images. They're like old photographs and I turn them over wonderingly. My uncle's strong brown hands scaling fish. The bamboo rod he made me that I wouldn't let myself use. His old tattered-eared cat asleep in a chair on the veranda. The sun on the water and the wheeling, shrieking gulls. A school of tiny fish trapped in a rock-pool. There was a little girl too. A little girl in a pink swimsuit. I played with her on the beach in the mornings. Once the fishermen had gone out, the beach was usually deserted. I was glad. I didn't want anyone to see me with her. After all, she was a girl and much younger than me.

I frown suddenly. I can't remember her name. She told me. I remember the solemn way she said it and then she laughed so her eyes crinkled up at the corners. It was the second or third morning. We'd been making a sandcastle at the edge of the water, I'd borrowed her spade to make a moat and she'd gone off with her bucket, collecting shells.

When she came back, she stood in front of me, her legs striped with dried sand, the bucket of shells swinging from her hand. 'You haven't asked my name,' she said. 'We can't be friends if you don't know my name.'

I didn't answer. She sounded too much like my mother. I pursed my lips and went on with my digging. All at once the water, laced with foam, swirled down my channel and into the moat.

'Hey,' I cried, jumping up. 'Hey, look at that.'

But she wouldn't be put off. 'I know your name. Your uncle told me yesterday. It's Nick. You have to know mine.'

I threw down the spade. 'Oh, all right. What is it?'

I can see us on the beach together, her eyes disconcertingly dark behind the tangle of her hair, but I can't hear her answer. It doesn't matter. Fifteen years ago. Two children and a pile of damp sand. A red bucket and a handful of shells.

I shake my head. I'm getting fanciful. It's the dark and the unfamiliar place. I should have at least waited until morning. I hear my uncle's voice in my mind. 'A fool's errand, boy, but no matter, no matter. What's done is done.'

I walk past a couple of darkened cottages. 'Summer people,' says my uncle's voice, full of contempt. The moon, sickle-shaped, comes out from behind the clouds and sends tree-shadows wavering across the road. Their branches look like tentacles. I hunch my shoulders into my jacket and move quickly on. Just ahead of me there's a girl. I don't know where she's come from. A cottage gate. A side street. She's all bundled up in an old overcoat but her hair, white as sea foam, tumbles over her shoulders. At the corner, she half turns and I catch a glimpse of her face lit by the single street-lamp. It's like I'm looking at it from under water. I hear a child shout, 'Sylvia. Sylvia,' and I'm running after the little girl across the wet sand. I stop, confused. Sylvia. Her name was Sylvia... But...but... The girl ahead of me isn't Sylvia. I know that. I know that because... At the edge of my mind something dark shudders and is still again. I clutch at a nearby fence to steady myself.

My uncle's cottage is on the other side of the main road. I take a deep breath and pick up my bag again. I start towards it. The girl's gone. Another side street. A gate to one of the lighted cottages. I don't know. It doesn't matter. She isn't Sylvia and even if she were… But, somehow, the loss of her is like a physical pain, like… Myself. I have lost part of myself. With a little incoherent cry, I throw down my bag and start to run back the way I've come.

She's making her way towards the beach. I'm suddenly very calm. It's all right. I can catch up with her. I know I can. For a moment I think I can hear her singing but we're on the path to the cliffs now and the wind takes the sound and changes it into the crying of gulls.

On the last day of my holiday, Sylvia and I came this way. Sylvia was running in front of me, laughing. I remember the wind then too. It blew her hair across her face like spray and she said, she said…

The girl ahead of me isn't Sylvia. I know she isn't. She can't be because…because…

I stumble and almost fall. I feel, more than see, the figure in front hesitate. 'You're going too fast,' she says. 'There's no need to hurry. Not now.' Her voice is thin and insubstantial. It's a child's voice, a little girl stumbling across the rocks trailing a piece of seaweed. 'Wait. Wait for me, Nicky,' she shouts. 'You don't have to be in such a hurry.'

I look behind me. The lights of the town beckon. Stars, they are like stars. A lost sailor, he can navigate by the stars, my uncle told me that and I…I… But it's too late. The girl ahead is inexorable. She won't let me go. Not now. I have to follow her. I have to follow her even though…

Ahead of us is the edge of the cliff. Below us, I can see the treacherous water, dark as molten lead. The girl pauses and turns to me. The wind catches her luminous hair and blows it across her cheeks and, my breath shuddering in my throat, I reach out a hand to touch it. 'Sylvia,' I whisper. 'Oh, Sylvia.'

She sighs then and looks away. 'I'm sorry, Nick,' she says. 'Really sorry. I waited as long as I could but I can't bear it any longer, all these years by myself and…and the cold, Nick. I wouldn't mind so much if it wasn't so cold and you…' Her voice quivers uncertainly. 'You…you don't mind do you? I mean, you said…you said we were friends and you asked me my name and friends, friends are meant to be together, aren't they?'

I try to speak then but I can't. There are too many feelings inside me.

Just before I fall, I remember everything. I remember her taunting me because I was afraid to climb down the cliff-face with her. 'If you're so brave,' I shouted, 'you go,' and I pushed her. I didn't mean it. How could I? I was nine years old and all summer I had been angry…

But it's all right now. Sylvia and I are falling together. She has hold of my hand and she's laughing. Above us, the gulls wheel in the suddenly blue sky and I can see my uncle's boat far out on the horizon. The light on Sylvia's hair almost blinds me. I can feel it swirling around us like water. Oh, the light, the light, it takes us and tumbles us over and over until at last we are lost in it.

At the Beach

Carlie's head breaks through the surface of the water and she comes up gasping. She glares at Min. 'You ducked me,' she says. 'I wasn't looking and you came over and held me under and wouldn't let me up.'

Min shakes her head. 'I don't know what you're talking about,' she says. 'I wasn't even near you. No one was.'

Carlie narrows her eyes. 'You're lying, Min,' she says slowly. 'I know you are. I was swimming and you came up behind me and you ducked me. And now.' She tosses back her wet hair. 'And now you have to let me duck you too. That's only fair. Otherwise…otherwise, I'll tell.'

'No.' Min's voice drops to a whisper. 'I didn't, Carlie. Really, I…'

Carlie smiles. It's a secret, oddly triumphant smile. Min flinches from it. She turns and stumbles, half-falling, through the water. Her heart starts to beat very fast. She's frightened. Carlie's stronger than she is. At any moment, she expects to feel Carlie's hands on her shoulders, feel Carlie tripping her, holding her under. And then…and then Carlie will say it was an accident. Her pale eyes will be wide and innocent and everyone will believe her. Last week, last week when they were riding their bikes and Carlie deliberately swerved in front of her so she fell skinning both her knees, Min had tried to tell Mum what had happened but Carlie, indignant, said she was lying. And Mum had believed her. She had put her arm around Carlie and smoothed back her hair when all the time it was Min who'd been hurt. And afterwards, afterwards when they'd been alone in Min's room… Min shudders remembering Carlie's face and the sudden menace in her voice when she whispered, 'You shouldn't have done that, Min Forrester, tried to get me in trouble with your mother. Now I'll have to get you back.'

At last Min's in the shallow water; it's easier, the wet sand, and then she's running, running along the beach. Carlie's shouting after her, she's laughing too but the wind takes it all and mixes it with other sounds, gulls and shrieking children and the music from someone's radio.

Min takes a deep breath. She's safe. The jetty is there. People. A spiky-haired girl with a baby in a stroller. Two boys and a man fishing, the sun gleams on their lines as they reel them in, a fish perhaps…

Min turns away and watches a crowd of little kids building sandcastles at the water's edge. The sea's flat calm. She leans against a pylon. The surface of the water is like polished metal. Not really blue at all except at the edge where the little waves make white scallops of lace.

All at once Min feels cold. She moves out of the shadow of the jetty and goes to sit in the sun. She leans forward and pokes her fingers in and out of the warm sand.

She doesn't like Carlie. She hasn't liked her for a long time. It had been all right to begin with. Mum had been so enthusiastic. She'd come home from the community centre and told Min she'd found a friend for her. 'There was someone new at craft today,' she'd said. 'Rose Collins. She's got a daughter the same age as you, Min. She even goes to your school. They've just moved here. Carlie doesn't know anyone yet. I don't suppose you've noticed her, though, she's a year ahead of you, she's skipped a grade. Rose says it's made the other girls a bit suspicious of her. Girls can be very cruel sometimes.'

Min had nodded though she didn't know then what Mum meant.

'You and Carlie are practically twins,' Mum had gone on, beginning to slice tomatoes for a salad. 'Isn't that amazing, Min? She was born on the seventh of September just one day after you.'

It had been fun at first, being twins with Carlie.

'You even look like me,' Carlie said, frowning at their reflections in the mirror. 'See, our faces are the same shape. If you grow your hair long and part it on the side like mine, nobody will be able to tell which of us is which.' She wrinkled up her nose. 'We'll be able to play all sorts of tricks on people.'

Mum helped. She made each of them a denim dress. Looking at the dresses side by side on her bed, Min had felt the first quiver of apprehension. Being Carlie's twin was a bit like being her shadow. But everyone else, Mum, Dad, her brother Ty, Carlie's parents, they all thought it a joke. They used to deliberately confuse them. Once, Min even went home to Carlie's place and spent the evening there pretending to be her while Carlie read Min's books in Min's room. 'Though I must say,' Carlie told Min afterwards. 'It's very boring being you.'

Remembering, Min sighs. She smoothes out a patch of sand and carefully writes her name .Miranda Forrester. Miranda Jane Forrester. She shakes her head. It looks wrong. She frowns and writes Min instead. She turns her head. A man is coming down the jetty steps. He's got a little white dog on a lead. Min hunches up her knees and lays her cheek against them. Her hair, darkened by the water, falls across her face. It looks like tangled seaweed.

The man with the dog is standing in front of her. She can see his thongs and his bare legs and his blue striped shorts. The little dog prances round him barking.

'You all right, love? You look upset. Is something wrong?'

Min looks up through her hair. The man's frowning. He's got a nice face, though. Glasses. Fat pink cheeks. Ordinary. Sort of like her Dad. All her life, Min's been told not to talk to strangers. Particularly men, men by themselves. Carlie's got a thing about it. 'Depends on the stranger,' she says airily. 'Any fool knows that.' But Min isn't so sure. She turns her head away and starts playing with the sand again.

The man hesitates but then he goes away and Min's relieved. But she's sorry too. She wishes she could have spoken to him. She wishes he'd sat down next to her and put his arm around her. She needs to tell someone. Someone who'll listen. Because she isn't Carlie's twin. She isn't even her friend. She's twelve now. She wants to be her own person. And she isn't. All of them, Ty, her mother, her father, Carlie's parents, even the kids at school, they've made it so she's part of Carlie, Carlie-and-Min. And lately…

'Carlie's weird,' whispers Min, letting a handful of sand slide through her fingers. 'I don't want to do what she says, spend all my time with her. I want…' She takes a deep breath. 'Miranda,' she says aloud. 'I want to be Miranda.' It's as though she's broken a spell. She's surprised. And suddenly she knows what to do. It's easy. All she has to do is go home. Now. By herself

Min jumps up and runs back along the beach to where she's left her things.

Carlie's there. She's sitting on her towel, rubbing sunscreen onto her legs. 'Hi,' she says, smiling. 'Where have you been? You wanna go get a drink or something?'

Min doesn't answer. She grabs up her bag and heads for the changing sheds. She goes inside. It's not a proper shed, just concrete walls open to the sky. There isn't anyone else there. Min shrugs off her bathers and pulls on her shorts and T-shirt. Then she scrabbles in the bottom of her bag for her comb. Behind her, she hears someone come in and, even without turning, she knows it's Carlie.

Carlie's panting as if she's been running. 'Wait up, Min,' she says. 'What's going on? What are you getting dressed for? We don't have to go yet. My mum said I didn't have to be home till four and you know your mum doesn't worry so long as you're with me.' She giggles. 'She thinks I'm responsible.' When Min doesn't answer, she adds quickly, 'C'm on, Min. I didn't mean anything before. I was just teasing you.'

Min tightens her mouth and goes on working at the tangles in her hair.

'We haven't even had lunch yet and I want to walk along the jetty and…'

'I'm going home,' says Min, putting her comb away and tucking her hair behind her ears. 'I don't like the beach much. I never have. I'd rather go to the park and read my library book.'

'But that's so boring. Only little kids…'

Min doesn't say anything. She pushes past Carlie and out through the open doorway. The sun on the water is very bright. She glances at it, nodding, and then sets off for the steps, her beach bag bouncing jauntily against her bare legs. .

Brothers

Ebony was Nick's little brother. 'You have to be,' he told her. 'There's no one else. Tegan's no good – she cries too much and, besides, she's scared of spiders. And Kate,' he made a grimace of disgust, 'Kate's gone real stupid – all she does is look at herself in the mirror. You'd think by now she'd know what she looks like.'

Ebony nodded. She always agreed with Nick. They were making bows and arrows so they could hunt the magpie.

'We've got to do something. It's got so vicious,' Nick said, carefully bending a length of willow and tying it taut with binder twine. 'Yesterday it swooped on Tegan and made her head bleed.' He held the finished bow out for Ebony's inspection. 'I'll make yours smaller, okay? But we'll share the arrows.'

Ebony watched Nick sharpen a handful of sticks with his pocketknife. She pulled off the ribbons that tied her plaits. 'We ought to decorate the ends,' she said, offering them to Nick. 'Otherwise they'll be too hard to find in the scrub.'

Nick frowned. 'Mum'll be cross,' he warned but Ebony just shrugged.

She screwed up her eyes and squinted into the sun. 'Feathers,' she said dreamily. 'Didn't they put feathers on arrows in the olden days? We'll have bits of red ribbon instead.'

Nick approved. You had to admire Ebony. She had real imagination.

Nick and Ebony did everything together. On Saturdays, when Mum and Kate and Tegan went shopping, Dad took them to soccer. Of course they played in different teams because Ebony was still only an under-eight but they wore the same colours and had the same opponents.

'Enemies,' said Ebony, tying her boots and looking fierce.

Nick tried to set her straight. 'You can't say that. They're all right. They're just on the other team.' But Ebony wouldn't listen so in the end he gave up.

The results of the matches were published in the local paper. Once, they were both chosen best player.

'Look at that,' Nick said, showing Ebony. 'People will think E. Barrett is N. Barrett's little brother.'

Ebony giggled. 'They'll probably think my name's Edward,' she said and she made Nick cut the piece out of the paper.

He was glad he did. He liked looking at it. It reminded him of something his mother had said years ago when she'd found him crying because he only had sisters. 'What could a little brother do that Ebony can't?' she'd asked. And she had been right. Ebony was the perfect little brother. Even better than a real one. Jonesy, at school, had a little brother who was a proper sook and all the boys teased him. You didn't have to worry about that with Ebony. She never cried, not even when she fell off her bike and skinned both knees.

The summer he was eleven and Ebony nearly nine, they joined the gang. It was innocent enough. Just a few of the older boys who were making a BMX track in the scrub.

Jonesy caught up with them on the way home from school and nonchalantly extended the invitation. 'Not her, though,' he said, his eyes flicking towards Ebony.

Ebony glared at him. 'Why not?' she demanded.

'Well…er…the initiation. You'll never pass the initiation. You're too young.'

Ebony narrowed her eyes. 'I'm older than your brother Shane. Did he pass?'

Jonesy flushed. He didn't want to admit that the only reason Shane was in the gang was because their mother insisted. 'Take him with you or you both stay home,' she'd said and Jonesy knew better than to argue.

While he was trying to think of something to say to Ebony, Nick interrupted. 'If she passes the initiation, will you have her? Otherwise I won't join either.'

Ebony flashed him a quick, grateful glance, then she confronted Jonesy again, her little sturdy legs wide apart, her hands clenched by her side. 'I'll do the initiation first, before Nick,' she said with tilted chin. 'Just to show you.'

Jonesy tried to look indifferent. 'You have to touch the electric fence

– the one round Sawley's bull. And not just touch. You have to grasp it with your whole hand.'

Nick gasped. He looked anxiously at Ebony but her gaze never faltered.

'Okay,' she said. 'Do you want me to do it now?'

'No,' said Jonesy. 'The others have to be there too. Witnesses, you know. 'Sides, you need time to think about it.' He grinned. 'Saturday morning'll do. Meet me at my place, half past nine.'

On the way home, Nick said. 'We don't have to. We can ride our bikes by ourselves.'

'No,' said Ebony. 'I want to join. A proper track'll be heaps of fun.'

'But the fence…'

'Who cares about that? It'll only be a minute or two. When my ear gets bad, it hurts for hours. The fence can't be worse than that.'

Nick grunted. Truth to tell, he was feeling apprehensive. He wasn't at all sure he could grasp the fence without flinching. And it'd be so embarrassing if Ebony did. He sighed. Sometimes it was hard having a little brother to live up to.

Saturday morning, her mouth in a tight line, Ebony marched up to Sawley's fence and grabbed it with both hands.

Jonesy gave a little gasp of admiration. He turned to Alisdair and Trent, nodding, as if Ebony had somehow enhanced his own reputation. 'Told you she was something else, didn't I?' he said smirking. 'Proper little tough nut.'

The other boys milled around Ebony, loudly congratulating her and slapping her on the back.

In all the confusion, no one seemed to notice that Nick never got to touch the fence at all. Afterwards he felt ashamed to have got off so easily. He crept back in the evening to undertake his initiation alone. He felt he owed it to Ebony.

Nick wasn't exactly sure when things began to change. Perhaps it was Carlie Spence's party. Ebony had never had much time for other girls but the year she was in Grade Five, Carlie had a big birthday party and invited all the girls in her class.

'My mother said I had to invite you too.' Carlie dropped the dainty pink envelope on Ebony's desk. She tossed her head. 'Of course I don't expect you to come. There won't be any boys there.'

Ebony put the invitation in her bag and forgot about it.

Unfortunately, Mum met Mrs Spence at the supermarket. 'Of course you'll go,' she told Ebony when she got home. 'It's time you started making friends of your own.'

Ebony opened her mouth to protest but then she shrugged. 'All right,' she said.

Nick stared at her. It wasn't like Ebony to give in so meekly.

Mum made over one of Kate's dresses. It was a dark maroon with a dropped waist and a wide white collar. Ebony looked surprisingly tall in it. Nick could hardly recognise her. Her hair, newly washed, was loose on her shoulders and curled slightly around her face. Her eyes, darker than ever, seemed different too. As if…as if…Nick could hardly bear the thought… as if another, shyer Ebony was looking out of them, an Ebony who…

'Why, Ebony,' he said before he could stop himself. 'Why, Ebony, you're pretty.'

Ebony shrugged and turned away but not before he'd seen the colour creep into her cheeks. She was pleased. She liked being pretty.

Nick felt an odd clenching around his heart. He wet his lips and went into his room and closed the door.

But the next day, Ebony was back in her cut-offs and old T-shirt, her hair sensible again in plaits. Nick kept stealing suspicious glances at her face. And he was right. She wasn't quite the same. Her eyes were still… secretive…there was no other word for it…and the curve of her cheek… even her bare feet. Had she always had such delicate little feet and her hands…

'Come on,' he said sharply. 'Let's get our bikes.'

That summer Nick was thirteen. There was a lot to think about. High school. It was more exciting than primary school but more difficult too. Not only the work, though that was bad enough. You had to be independent. He couldn't bear the way you didn't have your own desk any more. You had to shift from classroom to classroom. He felt… That was the trouble. He had no words to describe his confusion.

And the worst thing, the worst thing of all, in this different, frightening world, there was no place for Ebony. A high school boy didn't hang around with his little sister. The other boys were so much bigger than he. They, all of them, knew where they were going. They exuded confidence. He had to fit in. No matter what. He daren't risk their scorn even if it meant…

One night Ebony was waiting for him at the bus stop, the end of one plait in her mouth, her legs placed either side of her bike. He ignored her. He even crossed the road so he wouldn't have to walk past her.

'Nick,' cried Ebony. 'Nick, wait up.' She ran after him, panting, her bike lurching clumsily at her side.

'Go away,' he hissed, hoping the other boys hadn't noticed her. For one moment he let himself see her white, stricken face but then he hurried on. He couldn't allow himself to weaken.

After tea, Mum came into his room. She stood by his desk where he was pretending to do his homework and fiddled for a while with his pencils. Then she said, 'What's wrong with Ebony? She's crying.'

He didn't answer. Mum sat down on his bed. 'Ebony thinks the world of you. You know that. She can't understand why you don't do things with her any more.'

'There's no time. I've got all this homework.'

'Oh, Nick,' his mother said sadly. 'Oh, Nick.'

Desperate, he cried out, 'Ebony's a girl.' He thought for a moment he was going to burst into tears and he bit down savagely on his bottom lip.

'She's always been a girl.'

'Yes.' Nick got up and began re-arranging the Lego models on his chest of drawers. 'Yes. But before it didn't matter and now it does.' He whirled around to face his mother, daring her to contradict him.

But his mother didn't say anything. She sighed. Then she reached out and laid her hand against his cheek. 'Oh, Nick,' she said again.

She understood. She had always understood. Only, only before, she'd always been able to comfort him, to… Years ago, when Kate had started school, he'd been heartbroken. Mum had lifted Ebony out of her cot and said, 'It's true Kate's gone to school but you've got Ebony instead.' She'd put Ebony in his lap and Ebony had put her fat little arms around his neck…

But Mum couldn't do anything now. He was growing up. He had to sort things out for himself.

He said suddenly, 'I think I'll pack my Lego away. I'll need the space here for my books.'

Mum frowned. 'Are you sure? I mean…' Then she nodded. 'Yes, I expect you're right. I'll find you some boxes.'

Ebony came in a few minutes later. 'Mum said to give you these,' she said, dumping a pile of shoeboxes on his bed. She hesitated a few moments and then asked matter-of-factly, 'Do you want me to help you?'

He had hurt her badly and he knew it and was sorry but there was nothing he could do. She met his gaze without flinching. He turned away. Everything she was, was there in her eyes. It made his heart turn over. 'Fortitude,' he whispered to himself. 'She accepts things with fortitude.' He set his lips resolutely. After all, he was her brother. He could do the same.

'Here,' he said, his voice husky. 'You can dismantle this space station if you like. It ought to have a box to itself.'

Silences

There's a new boy. Carrie finishes putting her books on her desk and scrunches up her eyes to stare at him. He's standing by the teacher's table, his shoulders hunched as if, by not looking at any of them, he can hide himself. Carrie frowns. He's got his head turned away so she can't see all of his face but she can see his mouth. He doesn't like them. Carrie feels her own mouth go tight. It's more than that. He despises them. All of them. Even the teacher, Miss Fife.

Miss Fife's determined to be friendly. 'Andrew, isn't it?' she says, putting an arm around him. 'You're new to Australia, aren't you? Perhaps you'd like to tell us a bit about yourself before you sit down.'

The boy's head goes up. 'Andreas,' he says. 'That is the way it is said in my country. That is my name. Andreas.' Then his mouth quivers and he shrugs. 'It does not matter. You are right. I am here now.' His hands fall to his sides but his head is still up and his eyes, wide and dark, look beyond them to something only he can see.

Miss Fife nods and indicates the empty desk where he is to sit. The boy goes over to it. He walks like a soldier, Carrie thinks, biting at her lip, sort of proud and…and controlled, not like a boy at all but…he walks like a man, determined, she decides, and for some reason she feels an odd wrenching of her heart and she turns her attention quickly to the books on her desk. She isn't interested in boys anyway. Animals, they're like wild animals. They push and shove and shout at one another. Once, coming home late from school, she saw two of them fighting in the street. She was frightened then. Not of the boys. Of the feelings inside her. She couldn't sort them out. Horror and pity and contempt and something else too. A hot, sick excitement.

Carrie sits next to a boy of course. She has to now she's at primary school. She sits next to Wassel. She doesn't mind him. It could have been worse. Much worse. She could have ended up next to Gary, who's spiteful and hates girls, or Paul, who's thin and pale and smells sour.

Wassel's different from the other boys. Carrie doesn't mind him, though he's never spoken to her, not even a whisper when the teacher's not looking. He's like Andrew. He isn't Australian. Carrie knows it's because of the war. Now it's over, lots of people are coming to Australia to start new lives. Her mother explained it to her but Carrie's never really understood about the war. It ended just before she was born but in a way it hasn't ended at all because Carrie's father hasn't come back. He wasn't killed, Carrie knows that, but he hasn't come back either, or at least not to Carrie and her mother. Perhaps, thinks Carrie drawing butterflies on the cover of her atlas, perhaps he's gone to another country too, to start a new life.

Wassel doesn't even look like the other boys. He's got a lot of thick, whitish hair and heavy-lidded eyes and his face is too flat. Carrie shrugs and goes on with her butterflies. It isn't important. What's important about him is his silence. It's got a quality of its own. Secret. Impenetrable. Carrie nods to herself and adds a pair of delicate antennae to her butterfly. It's a good word. It goes with Wassel's smooth, closed face. Sighing, she glances around the classroom but everyone's head is bent down over their work. They're busy copying maps of the world into their geography books. Carrie gives a little guilty start but she makes no attempt to open her books. She's too caught up in her thoughts. Andrew's got his own silence too. She looks at him from under cover of carefully lowered lids. Andrew's silence is different. It's threatening. It's dark and angry. Wassel doesn't care about them but Andrew hates them and he wants them to know. Carrie feels herself shudder and she clenches her hands. It comes to her then that she too is surrounded by silence only hers is full of noise. She talks a lot but most of the time no one is listening.

The term drags on. It's the last week. Monday. Carrie's got her things all ready on her desk. She looks down at them and bites at her lip. She wonders if she dare start reading her new library book, *Black Marigolds*. She's got it hidden on her lap, ready. She traces round the picture of the bedraggled girl on the cover.

Suddenly Miss Fife raps on the table with her ruler. 'Children. Children, will you give me your attention, please?'

There's something wrong with her voice. It's too high. Carrie looks up frowning. Miss Fife's face has gone very pale except for two red blotches on her cheeks. She holds in one hand a piece of paper that one of the Grade Seven monitors has just given her. It's edges flutter like the wings of a white butterfly.

'Children,' whispers Miss Fife. 'Something... There's something I have to tell you. Wassel. Your classmate, Wassel. On Friday...he was killed...' Her voice falters, steadies itself and goes on. 'He and Andrew... They were playing on an old bicycle Andrew's father had fixed up for them, when a truck... Wassel skidded in front of a truck, the bike's brakes didn't work and the truck...'

Carrie stops listening. Her chest feels so tight she can hardly breathe. Next to her is Wassel's chair... She stares at it. It's too close. She wants to edge her own chair away but if she does...the noise...in the suddenly quiet classroom the noise if she moves her chair away... Confused, she glances around her. Andrew's across the room from her. His face is very still. It's like it's carved from stone, his delicately cut lips, his nose, his wide unseeing eyes. she lifts her head and stares into his face. He can't see her. She knows what he can see. Wassel. The bike. The truck. She knows the picture of it will be inside him forever. She feels her lips begin to quiver and she forces herself to look away.

Miss Fife has started writing the week's spelling words on the blackboard. Carrie opens her exercise book and starts to copy them. Silence, she thinks. The silence that was Wassel has gone but it doesn't make any difference. Not really. Not to them, the children in 5F. They didn't know him. If Miss Fife hadn't told them, they might not even have noticed his absence. Except for Andrew. It matters to him. Carrie's breath catches in her throat. Andrew has taken on Wassel's silence as well as his own and the whole classroom aches with it.